Innerspace

By the same author

The Hood's Army trilogy

Earth Invaded
Slaveworld
The Liberators

The Star Pirates trilogy

Kidnap in Space
Plague Moon
Treasure Planet

STEVEN SPIELBERG'S

Innerspace

A novel by Nathan Elliott

DRAGON

Dragon
An imprint of the Children's Division
of the Collins Publishing Group
8 Grafton Street, London W1X 3LA

Published by Dragon Books 1987

ISBN 0-583-31274-8

Printed and bound in Great Britain by
Collins, Glasgow

Set in Times

1

There was the sound of metal trays crashing and glasses shattering. Shouts and curses filled the air. The door burst open and Lieutenant Tuck Pendelton backed out somewhat unsteadily. He was in his late twenties, dressed in a smart black suit with a white shirt and bow-tie. The cook appeared in the doorway, a big man dressed in white. He waved a meat cleaver at Tuck and jabbered furious oaths in a foreign language.

'Okay, okay,' Tuck said to him, backing off. 'Accidents happen. I was looking for the Reunion Meeting. Common mistake.'

The cook brandished the meat cleaver, then withdrew, the doors swinging shut behind him. Suddenly Tuck realized that he was in another room, full of people, mostly men. They wore smart tuxedos and they were sipping cocktails and talking. A banner hanging overhead read: SPACE PIONEERS REUNION.

Tuck looked around. All eyes had turned to him. Through the crowd he glimpsed Lydia, conducting an interview with someone. She glanced in his direction, but the crowds closed up, blocking her from view.

Standing directly below the banner were the guests of honour. There were at least a dozen of them, all done up in their Sunday-best outfits. They glared at him with disapproval. He gave them his best smart-ass grin.

'Well, lookee here,' he said. 'If we're not wall-to-wall with All-American Hero-types tonight. I see space-walkers and Moon-walkers and Earth-orbiters galore!'

The astronauts were standing beside a display of large rocket models which charted the history of the space programme. With their crisp clothes, erect postures and frowns they looked like real stuffed-shirts to Tuck.

'Hell,' he said, 'the most excitement *I* ever had was the time I landed a crippled F-14 with stubborn nose gear on the deck of a rocking flat-top in zero visibility.' He lurched towards the rocket models. 'But you boys have gone up in *these* babies. I envy you . . . I *salute* you!'

Tuck snatched a drink from a table. He tried to raise it to toast the astronauts, but his legs weren't working properly and he staggered back, bumping the table on which the models stood. A Saturn rocket teetered and collapsed, hitting another, which in turn hit its neighbour. They fell like dominoes, reducing an impressive display into chaos in a matter of seconds.

Several of the astronauts exchanged fraternal expressions. One of them, a ginger-haired man, glowered at Tuck with a special intensity.

'How you doing, Rusty?' Tuck asked as if nothing had happened.

'Why don't you get yourself a new act, Pendelton?' said Rusty. 'You're a disgrace. And give that crippled Tomcat story a rest. We've heard it all before.'

He made to walk away, but Tuck said, 'Hey, Rusty – '

Rusty turned back to him.

'At least when my moment of truth came, I didn't wet my flightsuit in fright.'

Rusty's eyes blazed in anger. He swung a punch at Tuck's grinning face. But Tuck, though drunk, had been anticipating it. He ducked and drove a fist into Rusty's midriff.

Rusty went reeling back into a table, which promptly overturned, scattering hors d'oeuvres. A small cheese tart in the shape of a crown ended up on Rusty's head.

Tuck began to laugh. Then he saw the other astronauts gathering around him, looking menacing. He stepped back, giving them a goading smile.

'C'mon boys,' he said. 'This is what you've always wanted, isn't it? A piece of Tuck Pendelton!'

Swiftly the astronauts grabbed him and dragged him back into the kitchen.

They flung him down on the floor. Tuck scrambled up, saw them ready to converge again. He snatched up a big metal pan lid, and raised it in front of him as a shield. There was a CLANG! as a fist collided with it, and one of the astronauts yelped in pain. Tuck swung a punch, knowing that the odds were against him, but determined to give as good as he got.

The fight was hectic but brief. Pans clattered to the floor, plates were shattered as Tuck battled against the inevitable. He flung punches out at random, often connecting, but he got as many back in return, one colliding particularly painfully with his left eye. Finally he sank down against a wall, accepting defeat. But he was pleased to see that he had managed to inflict some damage on all of his assailants. One of the astronauts was nursing a cut lip, another a bruised chin, a third

7

had a lump on his cheek. They wouldn't forget this fight in a hurry.

A burly black man entered and peered down at Tuck. It was strange to see him in a dinner jacket.

'Where's your uniform, Pete?' Tuck asked, working his jaw.

'Where yours should have been a long time ago,' Pete Blanchard replied. 'Hanging in the closet.'

'Don't worry, Pete, the wait is almost over. You know I've resigned my commission.'

Blanchard offered his hand to Tuck and hauled him to his feet. Several other people had entered, among them Lydia. She looked gorgeous in a stylish black satin dress. Tuck winked at her. She wore her press pass on her breast, and her tape recorder was slung over one shoulder. She did not look pleased to see him.

'Take him home, Lydia,' Blanchard said wearily.

Tuck allowed Lydia to lead him out of the hotel and into her car. As they drove home, he kept telling her how glad he was to see her, and what a bunch of party-poopers the astronauts were. Lydia said very little and Tuck began to wonder if she was perhaps annoyed with him for some reason.

His apartment had a good view out over San Francisco Bay, but inside the place was cluttered with old newspapers, meal cartons, cast-off clothes and all the other debris of a single man's life. Tuck could see Lydia surveying it all with dismay. She hadn't been to his place in weeks, and since her last stay-over he'd bought a Harley-Davidson that he was in the middle of renovating. It lay in pieces at the centre of the room like some exotic exhibit of modern art.

Lydia, used to his eccentricities, scarcely paid it any attention. But she was interested in the robotic arm which stood on the coffee table.

'Smoke?' Tuck said, pressing a button on the arm.

It immediately went into motion, flipping open the lid of the box of cigarettes which he kept on the table for guests. Effortlessly its metal fingers plucked out a cigarette and held it up.

Tuck knew that Lydia didn't smoke, but he just wanted to show off the arm. Lydia did her best to look unimpressed. Instead she picked up a cut-away model of a rabbit that showed its internal organs and its circulatory system. Pinned on the wall were colour posters showing various aspects of the animal's inner workings.

'What's all this?' she asked.

'Something new I'm involved in,' Tuck told her.

'Rabbits?'

'Yeah. Sort of.'

She gave him an odd stare. 'You resigned your commission to study rabbits?'

Tuck shrugged. 'I didn't turn my back on the Navy, Lydia. The Navy turned its back on me.'

He knew she didn't approve. They'd had the argument a few weeks ago, and he'd hardly seen anything of her since then.

'Have you seen your eye?' she said to him. 'You'd better get some ice on that shiner.'

Tuck went over to a mirror. The eye wasn't as bad as he had feared. With luck, there wouldn't even be a bruise.

'I've had worse,' he murmured, and then he saw Lydia moving towards the door.

9

He spun around. 'Hey . . .'

'I have to go, Tuck.'

'Not yet,' he said, going over to her. 'Please stay.'

She shook her head.

'Wait a minute,' he said. 'There's something I want you to hear.'

He hurried over to the stereo stack and slotted a cassette into the tape-deck. Immediately Sam Cooke began to sing 'Cupid'.

It was their song, they'd played it over and over on their first night together. That had been one of the best nights of Tuck's life. And one of Lydia's, too, he was sure. He could tell she was responding to the music.

'That's not fair . . .' she said softly.

He approached her again and put his arms around her.

'Don't go,' he whispered into her ear.

'I have to . . .'

'You don't. I want you here. With me.'

He began to cover her face with kisses.

'Tuck, I . . .'

'You wouldn't desert a man when he's down, would you? You wouldn't forget how much we mean to one another?'

He indicated a framed magazine article on the wall. The photograph accompanying it showed Tuck sitting in the cockpit of an F-14 Tomcat, helmet off, giving his best smile to the camera. The byline at the end of the article was LYDIA MAXWELL.

'You can't live in the past, Tuck,' she tried.

'Why the heck not?'

He kissed her again, searching for her lips. She tried

10

to struggle against him as Sam Cooke sung on. Then she gave in.

Tuck awoke to find himself hugging his pillow. From the next room there was the faint click of the front door being closed.

Tuck sat up with a start. Instantly his head began to pound. There was a queasy feeling at the pit of his stomach, and his eyes were hurting. He remembered the events of the previous evening, remembered how drunk he must have been. The hang-over was going to be a bad one.

He climbed from bed and saw a scrap of paper on the bureau. Doing his best to focus in the curtained gloom of the room, he saw Lydia's scrawled signature at the bottom. Then he managed to read the note itself.

A car tooted outside. Tuck yanked the sheet from the bed and wrapped it around his waist. Then he charged out of the bedroom, stubbing his toe on the door as he wrenched it open.

He hurried down the stairs as fast as he could go, stumbling like Hopalong Cassidy. He flung the front door open and saw Lydia approaching a cabbie who was leaning agaist his taxi. The Golden Gate Bridge rose up behind them in sharp relief.

Lydia was carrying her shoes in one hand and brushing her hair with the other. Tuck heard her call to the cabbie.

'I said to the man on the phone: "Don't honk your horn. I'll see him." '

The cabbie shrugged. 'Lady, all I got was an address, not a book of instructions.'

'Lydia!' Tuck called. 'Wait!'

She turned as he hobbled towards her as fast as he could, clutching the sheet around his midriff, holding the note in his other hand.

Tuck decided to try and play it cool.

'Hey, Lydia,' he said. 'What's going on?'

'Any bags?' the cabbie said to her.

She slipped on her shoes and said, 'No.'

'Lydia . . .' Tuck said impatiently.

'You know what's going on,' she told him. 'You read the note.'

The cabbie was interested. He nodded. 'Good. Nice clean break. Leave everything behind.'

'Yeah,' Tuck said to Lydia. 'I read the note.'

Lydia had turned to the cabbie. 'I don't live here,' she told him.

Now the cabbie nodded knowingly and winked at Tuck. 'One-nighters.'

'Hey!' said Lydia, insulted.

'Just get in the cab,' Tuck told him, 'and mind your own business.'

The cabbie looked disgruntled. He retaliated by climbing in and starting his meter.

Tuck's toe was throbbing and he grabbed it with the hand holding the note, hopping in front of Lydia.

'I read the note,' he told her. 'It's your Standard Farewell Address. I almost know it by heart.'

Her face went stony. 'Excuse me,' she said, and tried to push past him to get into the cab. But Tuck wouldn't budge. The cabbie revved the engine.

'What's this going to prove?' Tuck said to Lydia. 'I'm not going to change. I am who I am, Lydia. You know that – and you love me anyway.'

'You've got a high opinion of yourself!'

12

'So what's the point in going? I'll call you. You'll call me. A week from now, we'll be back together again.'

'No, we won't. Not this time. This time I mean it, Tuck.'

She said it with such conviction that he was taken aback.

'I don't get it,' he said. 'I got a little drunk. I made an ass out of myself. What's the big deal?'

Lydia stared at him, and he felt as if she was pitying a stupid child.

'Things are different now,' she said. 'I've had enough. It just hurts too much to be with you, Tuck.'

She slid into the back seat of the taxi. Tuck, perplexed, desperately tried a plea for sympathy: 'I stubbed my toe running after you, Lydia. You know . . . I think it may be broken.'

'Better your toe than your heart, Tuck.'

She slammed the door, giving him a last despairing look. Then to the cabbie she said: 'Let's go!'

The taxi roared off – wrenching the bedsheet with it. Tuck was spun around like a top, and the sheet went fluttering away with the taxi. Tuck, suddenly naked on a busy San Francisco street, hopped for the safety of his apartment.

2

Jack Putter stared at the mural on the wall of Dr Greenbush's examination room. It depicted a tropical paradise with palms, sun-kissed beaches and a foam-flecked blue sea. It was pretty enough, but the colours were a bit too bright for Jack; they made his eyes ache.

Jack hummed to the Muzak that was playing in the background, even though he normally hated Muzak. He thought he recognized the tune: it was something by Sam Cooke.

Dr Greenbush entered and turned a dial on the wall, silencing the Muzak. The sight of his white coat always comforted Jack.

'Okay, Jack,' he said. 'Sorry for the interruption. Now, where were we?'

Jack was sitting on the examination table, and he began to feel highly nervous all over again. He was convinced that terrible things had begun to happen to his body. It was all going wrong, in ways too mysterious to fathom. Yet at the same time he was anxious that Dr Greenbush might be getting impatient with him: he'd been there over an hour.

'I'm taking up too much of your time,' he said. 'I think I'd better go.'

'Nonsense,' Greenbush said magnanimously. 'Take all the time you want. Your regular visits are the cornerstone of my entire medical practice.'

He paused to glance at Jack's chart. The longer he

14

stared at it, the more worried Jack became. Did it reveal some horrible disease with an unpronounceable name that even now was in the process of striking him down?

'Okay,' Greenbush said. 'Let's review what we have: we've got nausea; we've got shortness of breath; we've got headaches – '

'*Big pounding* headaches,' Jack said.

Greenbush made an amendment to the chart. 'Excuse me. *Big pounding* headaches. What else?'

'My hair.'

Greenbush blinked through his glasses. 'Your hair?'

Jack nodded earnestly. 'It's a big problem. I've tried everything. Regular and Extra Hold. Aerosol and an unpressurized pump. It doesn't make any difference. Whatever I use gives me a rash and makes me sneeze. What does that mean?'

Greenbush peered at him with the expression of someone whose mind is boggling.

'It means,' he said slowly, 'that you're allergic to hair sprays.'

To Jack, this was a medical diagnosis of a major order.

'What can I do about it?' he asked.

'Stop using it.'

Jack was flabbergasted at the simplicity of the treatment. Greenbush smiled benignly at him.

'This is great,' he said. 'Isn't it? I think we're making real progress here today.' He touched his pen to his lips. 'Anything else?'

Jack shrugged. He wasn't sure he wanted to reveal what was *really* bothering him.

'You can tell me,' Greenbush assured him.

'*The dream*,' Jack whispered.

'The dream?'

Jack nodded. 'Want to hear it?'

Greenbush shrugged. 'It's not my field, but go ahead.'

Jack made himself comfortable on the examination table. Then he took a deep breath before beginning:

'Okay . . . I'm at work. I'm at the supermarket, working on the check-out counter as usual. The next customer is this lady with bright orange hair. She's wearing those pointy – you know – Harlequin sunglasses.' Jack demonstrated their shape with his fingers. 'With the little sparkly things in them. And a lime-green jumpsuit with a three-inch wide red vinyl belt.'

'Very vivid,' Greenbush observed.

'Yeah. I have the same dream every night.' Jack could feel himself getting hot at the very thought of it. He swallowed. 'Anyway, I'm passing her stuff over the bar-code scanner, and I don't notice it, but the computer's gone nuts and it's ringing up all the wrong prices. I mean, twelve hundred dollars for a can of coffee! So when I'm all done I look at the register and the total's like way over a hundred thousand dollars.'

Jack paused for another breath. He could feel his heart pounding in his chest, and his palms were sweating.

'So the lady says to me, real calm, "I don't carry that kind of cash on me, sweetie. Will you take this instead?" '

Jack could feel the terror gripping him now, and he clung on hard to the edge of the table.

'And she reaches down into her purse and comes out with this pearl-handled silver revolver. She points it at

16

me and pulls the trigger – and *that's* when I wake up screaming!!'

Jack knew that his voice had gone out of control, rising to a frenzied shriek. Sweat had sprung out all over his forehead. He grabbed a tissue from a box lying on the examination table and began to mop his face. Greenbush patted him on the shoulder and nodded.

'Jack,' he said softly, 'you know how I feel about you. I'm more than your doctor, I'm your *friend*. So listen to me . . . You're suffering from *stress*, Jack, the worst kind of stress possible. *Empty* stress.'

Jack peered up at him, the terror of reliving his dream fading only slowly. 'Empty stress?'

Greenbush nodded again. 'There's two kinds of stress, Jack. Empty stress and *focused* stress. Focused stress is when you really have something specific to worry about, some crisis, danger or simply a tough task that you have to tackle. Usually focused stress is good, it's helpful. It's the kind of stress surgeons feel when they have to cut a patient open from here to here . . .'

Greenbush pointed to Jack's throat, then ran an imaginary line down to his naval. Jack recoiled in horror, as if he was actually proposing to perform a similar operation on him.

'. . . and climb in there up to their elbows,' Greenbush was continuing, 'and hope to God they don't make that one fatal error – that one small, accidental slip – that ever so critical miscalculation – that results in years of costly, time-consuming, career-threatening lawsuits from the patient or the family who've survived him.'

Jack was consumed with terror once more, imagining

17

himself paralysed on a life-support system or a hacked-apart corpse.

'Anyway,' Greenbush said dismissively, 'you don't have that. Your stress is empty. Directionless. Counter-productive. Unmotivated.'

Jack trembled, watching the doctor's lips form every word. 'You mean there's no hope for me?'

'On the contrary, there's plenty of hope. What you need is *rest*. Rest and relaxation. Maybe a nice vacation. But no excitement. Got it?'

Jack was so relieved he almost leapt off the table and hugged Greenbush.

'Believe me, Oz,' said Tuck, 'I've done my homework. I could do this job blindfolded and backwards.'

Ozzie Wexler slipped a pen into the top pocket of his lab coat. He blinked somewhat shyly at Tuck from behind his glasses. In his eyes Tuck could see a combination of nervousness and excitement. The project had been his baby for several years, and now its time had come.

'Let's just review the "Neuromuscular Facial Response Experiment" one more time,' he suggested to Tuck.

Tuck glanced up at the window of the observation room, more interested in what was going on beyond it. 'Let's not,' he said.

A lab technician with a videotape camera on his shoulder entered the room. He pointed the camera at Tuck and Tuck eyed it suspiciously, as if it was a gun.

'I want a complete visual diary of the entire experiment,' Ozzie said to him. 'We're taping everything.'

Tuck decided to let it pass. 'It's your show, Ozzie.'

18

He went over to the window and peered into the main laboratory of Vectorscope. The lab was housed in a rather ramshackle warehouse-like building in one of the poorer quarters of San Francisco. At the centre of the lab a team of white-coated technicians were clustered around the pod, hiding it from view. Wires and cables snaked between banks of monitors and control-boards; stacks of equipment had been mounted on bolted metal shelving. Everything had a cobbled-together look.

Tuck removed a silver pocket flask from his jumpsuit.

'Stop the tape,' Ozzie said to the video cameraman. And then to Tuck: 'Is that really necessary?'

Tuck thought it over for a moment before pointing to the video camera. 'Turn that thing back on. You'll want a record of *this*.'

Then he went over to a sink and poured the contents of the flask down the plughole.

When he was finished he turned to Ozzie. 'Okay?'

Ozzie nodded. Tuck returned the now empty flask to his pocket.

'You're taking it anyway?' Ozzie asked.

'I have to,' said Tuck. 'It's my lucky flask.'

The big burgundy Ford was caught in a traffic snarl-up on the outskirts of the city. Inside, Pete Blanchard was talking to a studious-looking man named Dr David Niles.

'Hard?' Blanchard interrupted. 'Try impossible.'

Niles honked his horn at the driver in front of them who was slow in getting moving. 'That's why I want you to be there,' he said. 'To see for yourself. Then, if you're interested, the project's yours.'

Blanchard wound down the window and tossed out a piece of chewing gum. 'First amaze me. *Then* we'll talk about funding.'

The line of cars moved on for a while, then ground to a halt again.

'Damn this traffic,' said Niles. 'We're going to be late.'

'Just out of curiosity,' said Blanchard, 'who's your guy? Who's going to be your pilot?'

'Somebody you might know of,' Niles hesitated. 'Pendelton. Tuck Pendelton.'

Blanchard stared at him for long moments, not saying or doing anything.

'What made you choose Pendelton?' he finally asked.

'He had the right qualifications,' Niles told him.

'Such as?'

Straight-faced, Niles said, 'He was the only one we could find who's crazy enough to do it.'

Blanchard was not amused. 'Let me tell you something about Tuck Pendelton. He could have been one of the best. He was a fine pilot, exceptionally gifted. But he hates authority. Can't take orders. And likes to make up his own rules. Other than that . . . his attitude stinks.'

Niles looked as if this was news to him. He looked sick, Blanchard thought, sick at the prospect of having Pendelton at the helm now that he knew the worst.

'Don't look so depressed,' Blanchard said to Niles. 'The experiment is bound to fail long before Pendelton has a chance to screw it up.'

* * *

20

Tuck and Ozzie mounted the steps of the platform. The two halves of the protective shield were open, with the pod sitting at the centre. Tuck carried an aluminium briefcase. He was tense, but he liked that. It showed he was ready for the job which lay ahead.

Technicians stepped aside for them while the P.A. system broadcast a stream of data which formed a backdrop to all other conversations. Tuck stared at the pod.

It was constructed of tough fibreglass, but it resembled a deep-sea diving sphere with plenty of adornments – stabilizers, rotors, thrusters, two mechanical articulating arms and a pair of floodlights mounted on top of the craft above the viewing dome. Inside was a cramped cockpit, with just a single chair.

The pod's preparations were hastily completed, a long hiss marking the filling of the air tanks. The batteries were charged, the fuel lines had been tested, all mechanical parts had been given a final lubrication.

Ozzie turned to address the video cameraman, who was still stalking them: 'We are using the experimental Kraken II Submersible Pod,' he announced. 'It's modified with a fifty-milliwatt helium-neon laser scalpel.'

'Zero minus five,' the P.A. system intoned. 'All personnel to their stations, please. We have zero minus five.'

Ozzie turned back to Tuck. 'Good luck, Lieutenant.'

The pod's hatch was opened, and three technicians helped Tuck inside. The project was so secret he hadn't talked to anyone about it, not even Lydia. But if it was successful, he might end up famous – more famous than any of the astronauts.

The hatch was closed over him and locked into place.

21

On either side of the pod were the two halves of the protection shield. Now Tuck could really feel the adrenalin surging through his veins. He was as ready as he would ever be for the experiment.

The technicians wheeled their equipment away from the pod. Tuck placed the aluminium briefcase to one side and strapped himself into the body-contoured swivel seat. The instrument panels surrounding him comprised computer terminals, keyboards, display monitors and numerous switches and gauges. It had taken him over a month to memorize their various functions.

The two halves of the shield began to draw together, closing around the pod like an enormous metal egg, leaving only a narrow gap between them. Tuck switched on the pod's interior lights, and the cockpit filled with a soft green luminescence.

'Here goes everything,' he murmured to himself.

Outside, Ozzie Wexler was seated in front of a bank of monitors which displayed interior and exterior views of the pod from a variety of angles. Ozzie consulted the clock, then slipped on a headset.

'Lieutenant,' he said, 'do you read me?'

'Loud and clear,' came Tuck's voice.

'Okay. Stand by.'

Ozzie leaned forward to adjust a dial on the control panel. A technician came up and said, 'Dr Niles isn't here yet.'

Ozzie gave a rueful shrug. 'That's *his* problem. We're going ahead as planned.'

'Zero minus three,' said the voice from the P.A.

Everything was ready. Ozzie gave all the instruments

one last scan. It was hard to believe that they were finally ready to take the plunge.

'Insert PEM Number One,' he said as casually as possible. But he felt a thrill at the words.

A robotic arm nearby reached out and plucked a silicon chip from its container with metallic fingers. The chip was like a small ochre cogwheel little bigger than a coin. With perfect precision, the arm fitted the chip into its slot on a bank of instruments.

'PEM Number One functional,' announced the voice from the P.A.

Ozzie found himself grinning. 'Insert PEM Number Two,' he ordered.

The same robotic arm now picked up a second chip and snapped it into a cylindrical circuit module. Two technicians then lifted the module and inserted it into the body of the pod itself through the gap in the shield.

'PEM Number Two functional,' announced the P.A.

One of the screens showed Tuck lowering a protective visor over his eyes as the laser grille aboard the pod began to glow brightly.

'Stand by for "Activate Centrifuge",' Ozzie said.

Tuck checked the buckles on his seat harness. A CLACK-CLACK-CLACKING sound began as the centrifuge was activated. Slowly the pod began to spin on a vertical axis. Brightening yellow light shone out through the gap in the shield.

'Centrifuge activated,' Ozzie announced for Tuck's benefit. 'Hold on to whatever you had for breakfast, Lieutenant. This is it!'

On the screen, Tuck was bracing himself in the cockpit. The pod was spinning faster and faster as the clacking sound increased pitch and gradually turned into a continuous high-pitched whine.

One of the dials on the control panel in front of Ozzie was labelled MOLECULAR RECLAMATION DEVICE. Ozzie turned the dial slowly but steadily, going all the way around. The whine turned into a shriek, and the pod was now spinning so fast that it had turned into a blur.

Ozzie and the other technicians lowered face shields similar to that which Tuck was wearing. The P.A. system, which had kept up a constant flow of informational chatter above the noise, now began to count down:

'Five – four – three – two – one – *Ignition*!'

The shriek had continued rising in pitch, and at that instant it ceased to be audible so that a shattering silence suddenly broke out. There was a flash of light, radiating inwards rather than out, like an explosion in reverse.

The technicians, watching from their seats, were sucked forward slightly. Styrofoam cups and papers swirled towards the centre of the laboratory. The silence was deafening.

Ozzie stared at the central monitor screen, which showed the platform on which the pod had been standing.

It was gone.

3

The security guard in the lobby of Vectorscope stifled a yawn and scratched his ear. Just as he was thinking that things were quiet, the doors opened and a small group entered, all dressed in blue overalls and peaked caps. They walked straight over to the guard's command station desk.

'Can I help you fellas?' the guard asked.

'Phone repair,' said the leading man. He was middle-aged, with grey-white hair. The guard thought dimly that he looked more an executive or scientist type.

The red light above the entrance to the labs was still flashing.

'You'll have to wait,' the guard told the men.

He looked puzzled as they delved into their bags and started putting things over their faces. *Gas masks*, he realized too late, for one of them had also raised a canister. There was a sudden hiss, and a gout of white gas was blasted into the guard's face.

He tried to rise, but felt his limbs going rigid. A blackness overwhelmed him and he slithered off his chair to the floor.

The group, all gas-masked and armed with canisters now, moved past the command station and pushed open the door to the labs.

They went down the corridor swiftly, purposefully, the white-haired man leading the way.

In the main lab, Ozzie Wexler extracted a pinkish

fluid from the end of the Molecular Reclamation Device with a hypodermic syringe. Then, very delicately, he took the syringe and emptied it into a shallow Petri dish which sat directly under the lens of a powerful electron microscope. Finally he put his eyes to the binocular-viewing eyepiece of the microscope.

He adjusted the focus, and the pinkish fluid swam into view. And there, floating in the middle of it, was the pod. Ozzie was still wearing his headset, and suddenly he heard Tuck's voice: 'I don't believe this . . . Oz? Can you hear me? I think you did it. I'm little. I'm shrunk right down to nuthin'.'

The P.A. system was rattling off details of air pressure, fluid density, molecular ratios, and much else. In the background, unseen by Ozzie, the repairmen entered the lab.

'Okay, Lieutenant,' Ozzie said into his headset. 'Now let's get you into Bugs.'

Close by, a white laboratory rabbit sat in a cage. It was Ozzie's intention to inject the pod – and Tuck – into the animal so that he could explore at first hand the creature's internal anatomy. Wires from various terminals were embedded under the rabbit's skin and connected to monitors and display screens. The rabbit's nose twitched nervously, as if it suspected what was at hand.

But Ozzie never had the chance to perform the experiment. At that moment the telephone repairmen stepped forward and began spraying gas into the faces of the technicians.

There was a moment of panic and confusion as the technicians tried to stop them. But very quickly their

26

movements slowed, their eyes glazed over, and they slumped unconscious to the floor.

Only Ozzie remained awake. He had retracted the fluid containing the pod into the hypodermic, and now he ducked down behind a bank of instruments, hidden from view. He put a handkerchief over his face and breathed slowly through it.

The intruders began to ransack the lab, obviously looking for data in the form of records, readouts and videotapes. It was clear to Ozzie that they were no ordinary criminals. One of them, slimmer than the others, seemed to have a better idea of precisely where to look.

The gas began to dissipate without having affected Ozzie. The intruders removed their masks and hats and an avalanche of auburn hair cascaded down the slim one's shoulders. Ozzie recognized her immediately.

'Margaret,' he breathed. 'Margaret Canker.'

He remembered her only too well, for he had been captivated by her stunning looks and forceful personality when they had worked together at another lab. Eventually she had disappeared from the lab under cloudy circumstances, and it did not entirely surprise him to see her engaged in a blatantly criminal activity. She was a brilliant scientist, but quite ruthless in her ambition.

'Look at this design,' Canker was saying to an older man with white hair. She indicated the paraphernalia of the control panels. 'Look at the waste, the inefficiency, the sheer *inelegance* of it all.'

Canker paused to study a piece of equipment more carefully. 'Here's the chip,' and she slipped it into an envelope. Her expression changed.

'What is it?' the older man asked.

'Something's wrong, Victor. Something doesn't make sense.'

She stepped back to view the equipment from another angle. Suddenly she turned and saw Ozzie crouching behind the instrument bank.

She showed no surprise but merely smiled.

'Well, well,' she said. 'If it isn't Ozzie Wexler.'

Syringe in hand, Ozzie made a dash for a set of doors, bursting through them and darting down the corridor. Behind him, Canker raised a two-way radio.

'Igoe?' she said.

'Yes,' came a deep gravelly voice.

'A man wearing a lab coat is about to exit this building. He's carrying a syringe. Stop him and recover the syringe.'

Outside in the Vectorscope car park, Igoe sat at the wheel of a black Mercedes 450 SL. He was a well-built, granite-faced man with black hair and glittering steel-blue eyes. He rested a black-gloved hand on the steering wheel of the car.

Moments later Ozzie burst out of a door and ran off along the shoulder of the busy highway next to Vectorscope. Igoe started the Mercedes and drove after him.

Ozzie glanced around and saw the Mercedes on his tail. He tried to flag down passing vehicles, but none of them stopped for him.. Finally he dashed straight across the highway and into a large shopping mall, leaving Igoe unable to cross the highway in his car.

Ozzie ran into the mall, breathing hard and sweating profusely. He still carried the syringe in his hand. The pink fluid inside it was sloshing around, and he reflected ruefully that Tuck was probably having a

28

rough ride of it in the pod, being tossed about like a ship in a stormy sea. But there was nothing he could do about that now.

Ozzie paused to glance over his shoulder. Just then Igoe's black Mercedes thundered into the parking lot and came screeching to a halt. Ozzie bolted again.

Inside the shopping mall, Muzak played softly and people strolled past, gazing into shop windows. Ozzie flung himself into a glass elevator. The doors immediately closed and the elevator began rising to the next level.

But, Igoe had caught sight of him. He swung up his black-gloved hand, the index finger pointing. Fire spat from the fingertip and a bullet smashed into the glass of the elevator.

A small boy was the only person who noticed. He stared at Igoe's smoking finger with amazement, then began to tug on his mother's sleeve. But she took no notice of him.

Inside the elevator Ozzie was unharmed. Igoe headed off swiftly to a nearby escalator which was carrying a line of people upwards. He pushed past them, striding up two or three steps at a time.

Ozzie stepped out of the elevator, trembling with fear at having been shot at. He huddled in a small niche next to a travel agents, peering around for a sign of his pursuer. There was none. For the first time since the intruders had burst into the lab, Ozzie began to think that he might get away.

Inside the travel agents, the man behind the desk was smiling as his customer made out a cheque.

'Congratulations, Mr Putter,' he said. 'I envy you. Fun, excitement, relaxation . . .'

29

Jack handed over the cheque. 'I'll take the relaxation. You can forget about all the other stuff.'

'It's a cruise,' the travel agent said. 'You get them all.'

'*No excitement*,' Jack said as firmly as he could manage. 'Doctor's orders.'

'Ah, but what about a little shipboard romance?'

'Well . . . as long as it isn't too exciting.'

Jack took a brochure off the travel agent, then left. He paused to stare at the 'Mexican Cruise' poster in the window, wondering if he had made the right choice of holiday.

A man came out of a camera shop opposite, fitting a new lens on to his Nikon. He looked around, and Jack smiled as the man snapped him, obviously wanting to test the lens.

Unseen by Jack or Ozzie, Igoe reached the top of the escalator. He spotted Ozzie immediately, huddling near the doorway of the travel agents, looking the other way.

Igoe raised his gloved hand, and once again a bullet spat from his index finger. It hit Ozzie in the back.

Ozzie lurched forward, colliding with Jack and putting his arms around him to support himself. Slowly he began to sink to the ground. He knew he was mortally wounded, and in desperation he pushed the needle of the hypodermic into Jack's bottom and pressed the plunger with all his might.

The man with the camera continued snapping them, amused by the display. Jack was mortified at the stranger who had suddenly grabbed hold of him. He felt a pinching sensation in one of his buttocks and immediately wrenched himself away, bolting for the down escalator.

Ozzie sank to the floor and lay still, the hypodermic rolling from his hand. Igoe walked calmly over and picked it up. When he saw that it was empty, he looked around for the other man. But Jack was gone.

The man with the camera was still standing there, now looking a little horrified. People had begun to converge on Ozzie's fallen form. Igoe walked quickly across and wrenched the camera from the man, who was too startled and too intimidated by Igoe's physical presence to do anything. Igoe headed for the down escalator as security men hurried forward to inspect Ozzie, who was already dead.

Igoe went straight back to his Mercedes. Alone inside the car, he pulled off his leather glove to reveal an artificial arm extending down from his elbow. Attached to the stub, in the shape of a forearm and hand, was an automatic pistol. He snapped it off and attached a more traditional prosthetic hand, then covered it with a fresh black glove.

He drove swiftly away from the shopping mall, travelling down the freeway for ten minutes before turning off on to a slip road which led to a modern white building in a quiet sidestreet. It looked sleek and sterile, one of the latest examples of functional modern architecture.

In one of the gleaming labs he found Margaret Canker sitting before a TV monitor. It was showing a videotape which had been stolen from Vectorscope. Igoe handed the empty hypodermic to Canker while Ozzie Wexler, on screen, addressed the camera:

'Miniaturization is achieved through the pairing of *two* 500-Series Photon Echo Memory Chips – called PEMs for short. The first chip is called a 'Controller'

31

and the second a 'Remote'. Only the controller is necessary for miniaturization, but *both* chips are required to re-enlarge.'

Canker pressed a button which froze Ozzie's image on the screen.

'I knew it, Ozzie,' she said. 'I knew it the minute I looked at your set-up. There are *two* chips.' She turned to Igoe. 'He used a dual chip system. You're sure the syringe was empty when you found it?'

Igoe gave her a full account of what had happened in the shopping mall.

'Wexler is dead,' he concluded. 'I made sure of that.'

'What about the other man? The one who bolted?'

'I never saw him before,' Igoe said. 'But I got some pictures.'

He put the camera down on the desk in front of her.

'We *need* that other chip,' Canker said greedily.

4

Tuck was lost in a maelstrom of confusion. First he had tried to radio Ozzie at Mission Control, but had got no reply. Then he had been bounced around, the pink fluid outside the pod swirling and bubbling as if someone was shaking it. It had made him feel positively seasick. He continued trying to radio Ozzie, but still there was no response. Then the shaking had stopped.

And something worse had happened.

Completely without warning, Tuck was slammed back into his seat by an unexpected burst of speed. He had been thrust forward, the tremendous acceleration causing him to black out.

When he finally regained consciousness, he was in another world entirely. It was completely dark outside, and he immediately switched on the pod's searchlights.

He found himself in a thick, soupy sea, travelling down a fibrous tunnel. He had no idea where he was.

'Ozzie!' he said again into the radio. 'Mission Control! Do you read me? Can anybody hear me?'

Nothing.

It was like being on the bottom of the ocean floor, travelling through a silty sea and glimpsing only vague details here and there. Wherever he was, the place seemed to be pulsing steadily, rhythmically, dull throbbing sounds echoing around the pod.

Then a cluster of globules appeared. They were

lighter in colour than the rest of the sea, and they moved like amoebae, constantly changing their shapes.

'What are these?' Tuck wondered to himself. 'Fat cells?' Was he already inside Bugs the Rabbit?

Something quite disgusting splattered across the viewing dome. It hung there for a moment like a lump of granular jelly, then slithered away.

'Mission Control,' Tuck said into the radio. 'What the hell's going on out there? I think I blacked out. Am I inside Bugs, or what?'

He waited for a reply. Still there was nothing.

'Ozzie, come in. Do you copy?'

Silence.

'What's wrong with this damn radio!' Tuck punched it with the flat of his hand, but he knew it was just desperation. There was nothing wrong with the radio, he was pretty sure of that. But there was something he could try to be sure.

'Ozzie,' he said, 'if you can hear me, I'm going to try to restore radio contact by activating one of these electromagnetic booster cells. Stand by . . .'

He punched a button on the glowing instrument panel in front of him. There was a loud BUZZZZ.

Jack, still trembling with fright after his strange encounter with the man in the shopping mall, hurried through the doors of the Safeway supermarket. Mr Wormwood, his white-haired supervisor, was waiting for him at the check-out counter. He made a point of glancing at his watch.

'Jack,' he said. 'You're late.'

'Sorry, Mr Wormwood,' said Jack, settling himself

into his check-out station. 'You wouldn't believe what just happened to me – '

'Tell me later,' Wormwood said firmly. 'We have plenty of customers who would welcome your attentions.'

A queue of people quickly formed, and Jack began passing their goods across the bar-code scanner. Wendy, an attractive young blonde, began putting the groceries into a bag.

'Wendy,' Jack asked her, 'do I look okay?'

She peered at him, turning gum around in her mouth.

'No,' she said bluntly. 'You look like hell.'

Jack raised his right hand. 'I'm still shaking.'

'What happened?' Wendy asked.

'I had a terrible experience – '

'Talk about terrible experiences! Have you ever tried Slam-Dancing? I went last night. Wow, never again.'

'Oh,' said Jack, 'so *that's* where you were.'

'Huh?'

'We had a date last night. Maybe you forgot.'

'Oh, yeah. I forgot.'

Jack stared at her with a mixture of longing and severe irritation. He had been trying to get her to go out with him for weeks and had waited for two hours outside a cinema before he had realized that she wasn't going to show up.

'You forgot,' he said. 'How could you forget? We work together all day.'

She munched on her gum. 'Look, Jack, I told you already, if you wanna be part of my life, then don't hassle me.'

Jack was baffled. 'Wendy,' he said, 'I'm *not* part of your life. That's just the point.'

Wendy simply blew a big pink bubble and popped it in front of him.

Jack turned back to his next customer. And gasped with amazement. She had bright orange hair and pointed glasses with bright flecks in the frames. She wore a lime-green jumpsuit with a wide scarlet vinyl belt.

It was the woman from his dream!

Jack began to quiver with fright. He swallowed hard, tried to calm himself. He took the first of her groceries and made to pass it over the scanner, little knowing that Tuck, inside him, had activated the electromagnetic booster at that instant.

The charge began to play havoc with the cash register. For a loaf of bread, it charged two thousand five hundred dollars. Six thousand for a tin of dog food. Fifteen hundred for a box of muesli.

Jack looked up and saw the figures glowing redly on the display. A paralysis of terror overtook him. The woman had noticed it, too, as had several other customers who were waiting. The total amount of the groceries was a hundred and twenty-eight thousand dollars.

The woman was staring at him. Jack could feel the blood draining from his face. Suddenly Wormwood arrived, glancing at the register, then at Jack.

Jack gazed blankly at him. This isn't real, he thought. None of this is real. I'm just imagining it all.

'Jack!' said Wormwood. 'What have you done!'

'It's a dream,' Jack murmured. 'I'm living my dream.'

One of the customers grinned at Wormwood. 'We thought you ran an honest supermarket here, Wormwood.'

'Boy, Jack,' came Wendy's voice. 'You really screwed up this time, didn't you?'

Jack scarcely heard her. He had eyes only for the lady with the orange hair and the lime-green jumpsuit. He tried to say something, but no words would come out. Terror was engulfing him, and he couldn't move.

'Listen, sweetie,' the woman said softly, 'I don't carry that kind of cash around with me.'

Alarm bells went off in Jack's head. *It was just what she said in the dream!* He saw her reach down into her purse. And pull out the silver pistol!

'Oh, no . . .' he said, closing his eyes.

There was a click. Then nothing. Jack opened his eyes and saw the woman lighting a cigarette with the flame that was coming out of the pistol barrel. He almost collapsed with relief.

'Jack!' Wormwood was saying. 'Jack! Get a grip on yourself!'

Jack became aware that he was positively vibrating with fright.

'I need some aspirin!' he gasped, grabbing Wormwood's lapels. 'Please! I'm begging you for an aspirin!'

'Unhand me, Putter!' Wormwood shouted, wrenching Jack's hands free and backing away.

Jack stared down at the array of groceries which he had just checked out. He spotted a bottle of aspirin. With trembling hands he picked it up, wrenched off the top and pulled out the cotton plug. Then he raised the bottle to his mouth and began to pour its contents into his mouth.

'Hey!' said the lady from his dream. 'I'm not paying for those aspirins now!'

'At eight hundred dollars a bottle,' said another customer, 'who'd want to!'

Laughter erupted. Wormwood tore the bottle from Jack's hand, the remaining tablets scattering everywhere.

'You're coming unglued, Jack,' Wormwood said. 'You're coming apart at the seams!'

Jack nodded his head at Wormwood as if to say that he agreed with everything he said. The anger began to fade from Wormwood's face, to be replaced by genuine concern.

'My God,' he said. 'He's completely spaced-out.'

'I'll handle this,' said Wendy.

She stepped forward and slapped Jack across the face as hard as she could. Jack's head spun around, and he was startled back into some semblance of normality.

'Come with me,' Wormwood said, dragging him gently but firmly from his chair.

Inside the pod, deep within Jack's body, Tuck felt the impact of the slap.

'Hell's bells,' he said. 'What was that?'

The pod swirled around for a moment, and then the disturbance subsided. Jack spoke into the radio:

'I hope you can hear me, Mission Control. I can't restore radio contact from my end, so you'll have to do it from yours.' He leaned forward to the control panel. 'I'm going to proceed with the experiment as planned. Phase One: Optic Nerve Interface.'

Anything was better than just hanging around, won-

38

dering what had happened. Tuck tapped the keyboard of a computer terminal.

'Okay, baby, show me the way.'

The pod's monitors could show sophisticated computer-graphic images created by combining information from on-board sensors with pre-programmed digital 'terrain' maps of a rabbit's insides. Together they produced a realistic three-dimensional simulation of the environment surrounding the pod.

But to Tuck's surprise, the screen remained dark. Then the words PLEASE WAIT flashed up in green.

'Please wait?' said Tuck, confused. 'Wait for *what*?'

Tuck's question was answered by the message which now flashed across the screen: ENVIRONMENT ADJUST REQUIRED.

Strange sounds started coming from within the computer to the accompaniment of this message.

'What is this?' said Tuck. 'I thought all the equipment in this baby had been checked out.'

He waited, drumming his fingers on the instrument panel. Lights blinked on and off, pulses and ripples passed across the screen. Then finally the monitor displayed a schematic map entitled CIRCULATION SYSTEM.

To Tuck, it didn't look quite right. He was sure it wasn't the same as that on the charts in his apartment. Then a synthetic computer voice broke his reverie:

'Pathway to Optic Nerve is as follows: Superior gluteal vein to common iliac vein . . .'

Outside the pod, there was a flash of orange light as the laser scalpel sliced into a vein.

'. . . inferior vena cava past right atrium to superior vena cava . . .'

39

The pod slipped through into the vein. Immediately a powerful rushing current swept it away. The liquid was straw-coloured, but it was packed with scarlet globules which moved with a life of their own.

'. . . to right internal jugular vein to optic chiasma,' concluded the computer voice.

The pod was in the bloodstream.

Jack sat in a chair in Wormwood's office, recovering. Wormwood stood over him.

'I know I lost my temper, Jack,' he said. 'I'm sorry. You've been like a son to me.'

Jack peered up at him, wondering. A son? Like a son to Wormwood?

'Well, a nephew, anyway,' Wormwood said hastily. 'You've got a big future in retail food marketing ahead of you, Jack, I hope you know that. I'd hate to see you throw it all away now by going psycho on us.'

Jack smiled weakly.

'How're you feeling now?' Wormwood asked.

'Better,' Jack assured him. He still felt like hell, in fact, but it seemed the polite thing to say.

Wendy entered, carrying a cup of coffee in her hands. Jack smiled appreciatively at her.

'Coffee,' he said. 'Great, Wendy. That's just what I need.'

She put the cup to her lips and took a swallow.

'I got it down the hall,' she told him.

At that moment Jack's eye started to twitch. He looked away from Wendy in case she could see the movement and might think he was winking at her. Not that he had any objection to doing so in principle. But under the present circumstances . . .

His eye kept twitching. Little did he know that inside him Tuck had steered the pod to the optic chiasma, where the optic nerves crossed to the opposite hemisphere on their way from the eye to the brain. To Tuck, the nerves looked like ropes as thick as a man's body. The whole landscape was weird, and Tuck was still amazed to think that he was travelling inside something living.

'Deploying Optic Remote,' he said into the radio, just in case anyone was listening.

Straight ahead of him was the softly shining hemisphere which was the back of the eyeball. The Optic Remote device was attached to a dart which was ready to be fired from the pod. Once planted, it would enable Tuck to see through the eyes of his host, no matter where he travelled in its body.

He punched a button, and the dart shot straight and true to its target.

'Optic Interface complete,' Tuck announced.

At that moment, Jack screamed and slapped his hands over his eyes. Wendy and Wormwood recoiled in alarm. Jack rocked back in his chair.

Inside the pod, Tuck adjusted the controls for the display screen. Still it remained dark.

'C'mon! C'mon!' said Tuck. 'Where's the picture?'

Wormwood stepped forward and gently pulled Jack's hands from his eyes.

'What's wrong, Jack?' he asked. 'Let me see.'

A black-and-white picture suddenly filled Tuck's screen. It showed Wendy and Wormwood peering straight at it with worried expressions on their faces. Tuck's elation at finally getting a picture quickly gave way to puzzlement.

41

'Wait a minute,' he said. 'Who are these people? Where's Ozzie? Where are the lab technicians?' He scrutinized the unfamiliar surroundings of the room in which the two strangers were standing. 'Where's the *lab*!'

The man began speaking, but of course Tuck could hear nothing. Why the heck was the guy talking to a *rabbit*?

'Okay now, Jack?' Wormwood was asking.

'I think so . . .' Jack managed to say. 'For a moment there, I thought someone had shoved white-hot sewing needles through the pupils of my eyes.'

Wendy looked revolted at the thought. But that was just how the pain had felt. Jack could only feel grateful that it had vanished as quickly as it had come.

'Go home, Jack,' said Wormwood. 'Start your vacation today and come back to us a new man.'

Jack could scarcely believe it. He nodded appreciatively.

'Thanks Mr Wormwood,' he said, then stood up.

Inside the pod, Tuck was still studying the monitor. As Jack got to his feet, the point of view displayed on the monitor also moved upwards rapidly.

'What the hell?' said Tuck. 'Did Bugs just stand up? Wait a minute. Can't be.'

'Mind if I use your phone first?' Jack was asking Wormwood. 'I'd like to call my doctor.'

'Sounds like a good idea to me,' Wormwood replied. 'Go right ahead.'

Tuck saw Jack's hand in the monitor as he reached for the phone. Only now did he finally understand where he was.

'I'm in a man!' he yelled. 'I'll be a sonofabitch! I'm

in a strange man, in a strange room, surrounded by strangers.' He paused to rub his chin before yelling into the radio: 'Ozzie, what have you done to me!'

Instinctively he pulled his hip-flask from the pocket of his jumpsuit. He uncorked it and put the bottle to his lips.

Empty.

He remembered only too well the performance he'd made of pouring it down the sink. He wanted to kick himself. He pushed the cork back in and returned the flask to his pocket.

'How the hell did I get inside a man?' he wondered aloud. 'I studied up on rabbits, not human beings!' He paused to consider what to do, and the answer became glaringly obvious: 'I've gotta *talk* to this guy, let him know I'm here!'

Working the instrument panel, Tuck punched up a graphic display of the middle ear. He punched in a pathway order, and immediately the synthetic computer voice announced:

'Pathway to middle ear is as follows: internal jugular vein to vestibulocochlear nerve to tympanic cavity . . .'

5

The screen showed a series of blow-ups of the photographs developed from the film in the stolen camera. Margaret Canker sat watching with Igoe as each image flashed up.

The first showed the hypodermic needle being stuck into Jack Putter's backside. The second showed Jack's face in all its flustered glory. The third showed the travel brochure in Jack's hand. The fourth showed Jack's supermarket name-tag attached to the breast of his shirt. Canker paid this final image particular attention.

'J. Putter,' she read from the tag. 'Assistant Manager.' She turned to Igoe. 'Find him!'

The pod floated into Jack Putter's middle ear. To Tuck, it looked like an enormous glistening cavity which completely dwarfed the pod.

Under Tuck's control, one of the articulating arms attached a small electronic device to the eardrum.

Tuck glanced at the screen which showed the view through his host's eyes. He was approaching the entrance to a building. Then he paused momentarily before continuing.

Jack had paused to scratch his ear in order to relieve a sudden tickling sensation deep within. Finally the tickling went away. He pushed open the doors, crossed a foyer and entered the elevator that would take him up to Dr Greenbush's office.

44

There were several other people in the elevator. Jack stood in a corner, keeping as far away from everyone else as possible. He didn't want to risk catching a cold or something worse before he went on vacation. The stabbing pain in his eyes still worried him enough as it was. What if he suddenly went blind in the middle of the cruise?

'Hello,' said a voice. 'Can you hear me?'

Jack looked around at the other passengers, certain that one of them had been addressing him, but they were all staring steadfastly at the elevator's closed doors as it carried them upwards.

'Respond if you can hear me,' said the voice.

Once again, Jack looked around. Once again, no one was looking at him or giving any indication that they had spoken.

'Repeat,' said the voice. 'Respond if you can hear me.'

Very hesitantly, and in a whisper, Jack said, 'Who? Me?'

'It works!' came the voice, very loudly and enthusiastically. 'I can hear you!'

Jack was thunderstruck, still not knowing who had spoken. The elevator pinged to a halt, the doors slid open, and Jack bolted out, escaping down a corridor.

He found Dr Greenbush's office, and gave his name to the receptionist. She told him to sit down, Dr Greenbush wouldn't be long.

Jack perched himself between a man and a woman who were both flicking through magazines. A feeling of impending doom had gripped him once more, and he wondered how much longer he could survive in such a constant state of agitation. If nothing else, his heart would eventually give out under the strain –

'Now that we can hear each other,' said the voice, 'I think we should have a talk.'

Jack went rigid, looking straight ahead. After several moments he turned slowly to the man sitting next to him. He did not look up from his magazine, but Jack studied him suspiciously.

'Are you listening to me?' said the voice. 'Do I have your attention?'

'Yes!' Jack said to the man. 'You have my attention! What is it you want?'

The man looked up, startled by Jack's outburst. Jack immediately began to regret his aggressive behaviour.

'I'm sorry,' he said to the man. 'I'm a little on edge today.' He forced a smile, baring his teeth. 'Were you talking to me?'

'No,' said the man.

'Please forgive me,' Jack told him. 'Return to your magazine.'

The man rolled his eyes, then started reading again.

'Don't talk to *him*,' said the voice. 'Talk to *me*.'

Jack was now certain that the man was deliberately fooling around with him while trying to look as innocent as possible.

'That's very rude!' he said. 'Throwing your voice in a waiting room! That's a very rude thing to do!'

The man looked up with a bewildered expression. 'What?'

'See?' the woman on the other side of Jack said to the man. '*Everybody* thinks you're rude.'

'Why don't you just shut up,' the man said to her.

46

Jack was baffled by this exchange, having assumed until now that the two were strangers to one another.

'We have to talk,' said the voice.

'No we don't,' Jack said to the man.

'Don't what?' the man asked.

'We don't have to talk.'

'Yes we do,' said the voice.

Jack glared hatefully at the man until he became aware that the woman was staring at him.

'What is it?' he asked her.

'Are you feeling all right?' she enquired.

'Would I be in a doctor's office if I was feeling all right?'

'You don't have to snap my head off!'

Jack began to wonder. There was something rather familiar about her voice.

'Say that again,' he requested.

'Huh?' said the woman.

'Say that again. Only lower your voice just a bit.'

The woman frowned, then shrugged. 'Well, all right.' She lowered her voice. 'You don't have to snap my head off.' She smiled at him. 'How was that?'

'A little lower,' said Jack.

In an even lower voice, the woman said, 'You don't have to snap my head off.'

'Ah-*ha*!' Jack said triumphantly. 'It's *you*! You're the one!'

The man leaned across him. 'I can't believe you!' he said to the woman. 'You're such a push-over. You'll do anything anyone asks – even a perfect stranger.'

'Drop dead,' she responded.

'Listen to *me*,' said the voice. 'Please! Who are you? What's your name?'

'Will you leave me alone!' Jack demanded of the woman.

'I'm not doing anything!' she insisted. 'What am I doing? Tell me what I'm supposed to be doing?!'

'I'm not out there,' said the voice. 'I'm *in here*!'

Jack turned to the man. 'There! Did you hear that? You're my witness. What did she say?'

The man considered. 'She said, "What am I doing? Tell me what I'm supposed to be doing?"'

'No, no! *After* that! *After* that!'

'I didn't hear a thing.'

For a moment Jack was shocked. Then he began to feel paranoid.

'I get it,' he said to both the woman and the man. 'You're both in this together, aren't you? It's a *conspiracy*, isn't it?'

The man simply glared past him at the woman before saying, 'We prefer to think of it as a bad marriage.'

'I told you,' the voice insisted, 'I'm not out there! I'm *in here*! In you! Right inside your body!'

Jack finally knew that it was neither the man nor the woman. There was no one else in the waiting room. A feeling of pure terror washed through him.

'Somebody help me,' he murmured.

The woman put a hand on his arm. 'What is it?' she asked softly.

Jack's voice cracked as he said, 'I'm possessed by a demon!'

When Dr Greenbush returned to his examination room, he saw Jack lying flat on his back on the floor with his legs raised straight up against the wall. Jack breathed loudly and slowly through his mouth as Greenbush squatted beside him.

'Good news,' Greenbush said in quite a matter-of-fact tone. 'I think we can rule out demonic possession right off the bat.'

Jack looked around at him. 'But this little voice is talking to me.'

Greenbush smiled. 'See? That *proves* it. Demons talk *through* you, not *to* you.'

Jack reflected on this. It brought no comfort. He said as much to Greenbush. Then he raised his arms until his fingertips touched above his head before slowly lowering them to the floor again. Greenbush was forced to duck to avoid being hit.

'Do you mind if I ask you something?' Greenbush said.

'Go ahead.'

'What are you doing?'

'I began to hyperventilate,' Jack told him. 'This usually does the trick.'

He took three more deep breaths, then sprang to his feet.

'Yeah,' he announced. 'That feels better now.'

Inside the pod, Tuck saw Greenbush on his monitor.

'A doctor!' he exclaimed. 'Thank God! A man of science! Someone who will understand!'

Jack instantly began to panic again.

'It's happening right now!' he told Greenbush. 'Hurry! I can hear the voice *now*!'

'Okay, okay,' Greenbush said. 'We'll check it out.' He produced his ear-examination light and raised it to Jack's ear.

'Please!' Tuck yelled from the pod. 'Talk to your

49

doctor for me! Tell him I'm in, uh . . .' He paused to glance at the computer display. 'Tell him I'm in the Tympanic Cavity!'

Tuck was certain that this precise anatomical term would capture the doctor's attention. He turned to look out through the viewing dome.

A brilliant, searing blaze of light flooded the pod. Tuck covered his eyes against its blinding intensity. But it was too late. As the light blinked out, he took his hands away from his face. But he could see nothing.

'Oh God!' he said. 'Oh God! I'm blinded!'

Greenbush withdrew the light from Jack's ear and switched it off.

'Sorry, Jack,' he said. 'Didn't see a thing.'

'You can't do anything for me!' Jack said desperately.

'Go home,' Greenbush said as gently as possible. 'Go home and try to get some rest. That's what you need most of all. Rest. Take a few of those sleeping pills I gave you. Then we'll see how you feel in the morning.'

Jack turned his Volkswagen into the parking area of a small apartment complex. Then he clambered up the stairs to his apartment.

Once inside, he collapsed into an easy chair, feeling frayed and utterly exhausted. He hadn't heard the voice since leaving Greenbush's office, but there wasn't anything very comforting about this fact. He was convinced that he had already started to crack up.

God, he felt tired. He closed his eyes, wondering if he could snatch a few hours sleep. At least it was quiet here. At least there was no one else to bother him –

50

'I CAN SEE!!' yelled the voice.

Jack shot up from the chair into the middle of the room as if someone had suddenly electrified the seat of the chair.

'Thank God,' the voice said, a little more calmly. 'I can still see.'

Jack was poised for an attack from any direction.

'Where are you?!' he shouted to the empty room. '*Who* are you??'

'Jack,' said the voice, 'we've got ourselves a strange little situation here.'

Jack was spinning around, peering into all the corners, all the nooks and crannies.

'It knows my name,' he muttered. 'Famous psychopaths down through the ages have all had little voices in their heads. And now I have one, too!'

'Jack, listen to me – '

'No!' Jack screamed. 'I won't! I won't!'

He clamped his hands over his ears as tightly as he could.

'Jack!' said the voice, quite undiminished in volume 'Please! Be sensible.'

'Sensible!' Jack began to snigger. 'This doesn't work,' he said, taking his hands from his ears. 'I know – I'll watch some TV.'

'No you won't,' said the voice.

'Oh, yeah? Try and stop me.'

Jack plucked the remote control device from the arm of the sofa and switched the television on. A game-show host was asking an elderly woman with a purple rinse a question about the San Andreas Fault. Jack turned the volume right up.

Inside the pod, Tuck grew angry. He hit the two Electromagnetic Booster buttons and held them down.

The game show and its sound vanished and was replaced by strobing white lines on a grey background and a loud static hiss.

Jack began to hit the buttons on his remote-control to try to re-establish the picture. But the static sounds grew louder and the strobing lines became more frequent, more startling. Then the telephone began to ring.

Jack snatched the receiver from the cradle.

'Hello?' he said into the mouthpiece.

There was no reply. And the phone was still ringing!

The videorecorder underneath the television suddenly ejected a tape with such force that it flew across the room towards Jack like a bullet out of a gun. Jack ducked and it hit the wall behind him so hard that it embedded itself in the plaster.

Jack put the phone down. Smoke had begun to billow out of the top of the TV and from the vents at the back. It began to fizz and hiss to the accompaniment of popping sounds.

Darting into the kitchen, Jack plucked a small fire extinguisher from its bracket on the wall. He rushed back into the living room and began to spray the television with foam.

At the same time, in the pod, the Electromagnetic Booster unit suddenly flamed out, causing Tuck to withdraw his fingers hastily. He grabbed an on-board fire extinguisher and doused the flames.

There was silence in Jack's apartment. Jack stood there, his fire extinguisher still at the ready.

'Jack,' said the voice, 'I think we've gotten this relationship off on the wrong foot.'

It was the final straw for Jack. He sank down into the sofa with an expression of defeat.

'I don't believe this,' he murmured.

'I am real, Jack,' said the voice. 'You *do* believe that now, don't you?'

Jack shook his head, but it wasn't a denial. 'I don't know what to believe.'

'Believe it, Jack,' the voice continued, 'because it's *true*. Did you ever see that movie where Tony Curtis and Sidney Poitier are handcuffed together?'

'Yeah,' said Jack, unsure of the relevance of this. 'I remember it.'

'Well, that's us, Jack.'

Jack was confused. 'What are you saying? I'm supposed to be Curtis? Or Poitier?'

'I'm saying we're in this together, and we have to help each other. You don't work at the lab, do you?'

'I work at Safeway,' Jack said.

'And you don't know anything about the experiment, do you?'

'What experiment?' This was ludicrous, talking to a voice in his head.

'A miniaturization experiment. My name is Lieutenant Tuck Pendelton, Jack. I've been placed in a submersible pod, miniaturized. I was supposed to have been injected into a laboratory rabbit.' There was a pregnant pause. 'Somehow I got inside you instead.'

Jack sat up, thinking about it. He had never heard anything so ridiculous in all his life.

'That's crazy!' he said. 'That's completely and utterly lunatic.'

53

'No it's not.'

'Of course it is. Even assuming such a thing was possible, why would anyone want to do that? Who would allow themselves to be *miniaturized*, for God's sake!'

Again there was a pause. Jack had the impression that the voice inside him –. or rather the person to whom the voice belonged – was mulling it over.

'What do *you* know about it?' the voice finally said, somewhat defensively.

Jack put the fire extinguisher down on the sofa. 'I know that somebody would have to be pretty desperate to volunteer for an experiment like that! I mean, hey, I'll donate my body to medical science – but not until I'm *finished* with it! How hard up can you get!'

Yet again there was a pause. But despite all his bluster, Jack suddenly found that he was convinced by the story. The whole thing was so preposterous it made a weird sort of sense in the absence of any other rational explanation. And to Jack it was a far better explanation of the voice he was hearing than the possibility that he was going mad.

'How big are you, anyway?' he asked.

'I think you mean, how *small*,' said the voice. 'Small enough to be injected into you through a hypodermic needle.'

Instantly Jack remembered the sting he had felt in his buttock in the shopping mall when that crazy guy had grabbed hold of him. That could have easily been a hypodermic.

'I need something to drink,' Jack said softly.

'Now we're talking!' the voice said with some relish.

54

Jack rose and went into his kitchen. From the fridge he removed a bottle filled with a dark red liquid.

'Is that wine?' asked the voice.

'It's prune juice,' Jack told him.

'Prune juice! You've gotta be kidding!'

'What's wrong with that? All natural ingredients. No chemicals or additives. It's good for you.'

'It's not exactly what I had in mind.'

'Who's having this drink, anyway?' said Jack. 'You or me?'

'With any luck,' said the voice, 'both of us. C'mon. Think of me as company. Be a good host and take out the hard stuff.'

Dutifully Jack looked through his cupboards. He tended to avoid alcohol, fearful that it might do permanent damage to his body. But finally he came across a bottle.

'Here's some sherry left over from Christmas,' he announced.

The voice murmured something, and it did not sound approving. Then, louder, it said, 'Okay, sherry's fine. Here's what you do. Take a nice big tug on that baby and I'll do the rest.'

Jack uncorked the bottle and lifted it towards his lips. Meanwhile Tuck, now positioned in Jack's throat, had activated one of the pod's articulating arms. It extended out from the pod's body with a soft mechanical whirring. Clutched in its claw was Tuck's empty flask.

Tuck looked through the viewing dome to make sure that the arm and flask were properly in place.

'Okay, Jack,' he said. 'Down the hatch!'

A few seconds later, a tidal wave of amber liquid splashed down from above, crashing into the pod. Tuck was flung back in his seat as the pod went swirling and tumbling along in the current.

It was a rough ride, the pod bumping and crashing against the sides of Jack's alimentary canal. At length it came to rest in a dark vestibular channel.

Tuck pressed a few buttons, and the articulating arm began to retract into the pod. Presently claw and flask slid into the pod through an air-lock opening.

Tuck took a cloth and wiped the outside of the flask before sloshing it around under his nose. It gave off a pungent odour.

'Hmm,' he said to himself. 'Smells a little like floor cleaner.' He peeked into the bottle. 'Looks a shade green.' But his desire for some alcohol overcame any reservations. 'Oh, well. Probably just some harmless biochemical waste material . . .'

He gave it a final slosh preparatory to putting the flask to his mouth. A drop of the liquid splashed out on to the breast of his jumpsuit. It hissed, fumed, and burnt a hole straight through the fabric.

Tuck stared at the flask with horror, realization dawning.

'Hydrochloric acid!' he murmured. The pod must have slipped down into Jack's stomach so that the flask had filled up with his digestive juices.

Swiftly he capped the flask and set it aside. Suddenly he heard a knocking sound from 'outside'.

'What's that?' he asked Jack.

Through his eyes, Tuck watched Jack go out of the kitchen and through the living room to open the door.

A man clad in black leather was standing there, holding something in his hand.

'Jack Putter?' he asked.

'Yeah . . .' said Jack.

'From World Tour Travel,' the man said, handing him the envelope. 'Cruise tickets, I think.'

Jack took the envelope. The man then handed him the clipboard he was also carrying. 'Sign on number twelve.'

Jack took the pen and signed.

'Mind if I use your phone?' the messenger asked.

'No . . . I guess not,' said Jack.

The messenger entered, and the first thing he noticed was Jack's foam-covered TV.

'What's up?' he asked. 'Thinking of giving your set a shave?'

'Just a small domestic accident,' Jack told him. He pointed to the phone. Turning his back to Jack, the messenger picked it up and began dialling.

'Lucky man,' he said conversationally. 'Going on a cruise. What about your room mate?'

'Room mate?' said Jack.

'Thought I heard you talking to somebody as I came to the door.'

'No, no,' Jack said hastily. 'I live here alone.'

'Don't trust him!' came Tuck's voice from within. 'He's not a messenger!'

Jack backed away, whispering, 'How do you know?'

'Gut reaction,' Tuck said. 'Call it survival instinct. Just *get out now*.'

The messenger muttered something into the phone, obviously not wanting Jack to hear. He hung up, then saw that Jack was looking at him strangely.

Jack glanced towards the door. The messenger immediately looked suspicious.

Panic overwhelmed Jack. He made a dash for the door, but the messenger was faster, leaping in front of him and blocking his path. He also drew a gun.

Jack instinctively grabbed his gun hand, and the two of them began to struggle for control of it. Locked together like a pair of arm wrestlers, they strained and heaved, strained and heaved.

Tuck had taken the pod into Jack's blood system. The pounding of his heart grew louder, and the pod was carried along faster and faster as the blood pumped through Jack's veins and arteries.

'Jack!' Tuck cried. 'Your pulse rate! I'm going too fast!'

With infuriating calmness, the synthetic computer voice announced: 'Approaching tricuspid valve of heart. Do not enter. Do not enter heart.'

Tuck stared at the monitor. Jack and the messenger were still grappling for control of the gun. It was raised in the air above their heads, all four hands wrapped around it.

Tuck, studying the gun, realized something.

'The safety's on!' he shouted at Jack. 'He can't fire it!'

The monitor suddenly went black. It took a second for Tuck to realize what had happened: Jack had shut his eyes in fright.

'Open your eyes!' he yelled. 'I can't see!'

Jack obeyed. Still he was locked together with the messenger.

'Bring your knee up!' Tuck shouted. 'Bring it up fast – NOW!!'

58

Jack did as he was ordered.

The messenger gave a grunt of pain and released his hold on the gun, staggering backwards in pain. Jack was left holding the gun by its barrel as the messenger doubled up in front of him.

'Hit him!' Tuck ordered. 'Use the gun as a club!'

Jack hesitated.

'Do it!' Tuck yelled.

Jack brought the gun down hard on the back of the messenger's head. He crumpled to the floor.

'Now run!' Tuck shouted.

But Jack was staring down at the messenger, 'I'm so sorry . . .' he began.

'Don't apologize!' Tuck screamed. '*Run!*'

Jack dropped the gun and wrenched open the door. Then he bolted, heading across the courtyard.

Just then he spotted a dark-suited man entering the courtyard. There was something familiar about him, especially his black-gloved hand. Before the man could see him, Jack ducked behind a palm tree, out of sight.

The man passed by and entered Jack's apartment. Jack could feel his blood running cold again. The guy had the meanest face, and it was a sure bet that he wasn't going around trying to sell people encyclopaedias.

'What's going on?' Jack whispered urgently to Tuck. His heart was still pounding at a terrible rate. 'Why are all these people after me, Tuck? . . . Tuck?'

Deep within Jack, Tuck was far too busy to answer. The pod was hurtling towards Jack's heart at a tremendous speed, caught in a rapid red flow. Tuck fought for control of the craft as it bumped along. The interior lights had dimmed, and the computer was flashing WARNING! on one of the screens.

Tuck pushed forward two console panel levers. Immediately the forward thrusters on the side of the pod fired up and began to reverse, fighting the current. The pod slowed, vibrating strongly under the strain. Dead ahead, Tuck could see the gaping maw of the heart valve. It opened and closed like the mouth of a giant eel. Still the pod was moving towards it.

Tuck deployed one of the articulating arms. It shot out from the pod, and Tuck manipulated the controls, trying to grab the side of the atrial wall with the steel claw at its end.

Tuck's head was filled with a roar of sounds: the thrusters shrieking, the valve pounding, the blood rushing into the heart. At the last possible moment, just as Tuck was convinced the pod was going to disappear down into the heart – the claw took hold of the atrial wall.

Tuck activated the laser scalpel and sliced an opening. Giving the pod full thrust, he pushed it through the gap to safety. Immediately afterwards he sealed the incision, using the laser at lower intensity to weld the muscle back together. Only then did he pause to mop his brow. His jumpsuit was soaked through with sweat.

Looking up at the monitor, Tuck saw Jack at the wheel of his Volkswagen, driving rapidly down a road.

'Jack?' he said. 'Are you okay?'

'Tuck!' Jack said with obvious relief. 'Where have you been?'

'That's not important,' Tuck told him, deciding to spare him the messy details of how he had nearly killed him. 'Right now we've got to get back to the lab.'

6

Jack sat in the Observation Room of Vectorscope, talking to Niles and Blanchard. Through the window he could see a team of technicians tidying up the lab beyond. It had been ransacked.

'He can actually talk to you?' Niles was saying to Jack.

Under Tuck's instructions, Jack had told both men the whole story. He nodded. 'Yes, sir. He can talk to me, and I can talk to him – and he can see everything that I see.'

Niles looked triumphant. 'He's patched into the optic nerve *and* the eardrum!' He turned to Blanchard. 'That was part of the experiment! To see if a miniaturized human could make visual and audio contact with his host organism.'

Blanchard gave a twisted smile. 'C'mon, Doc. We're talking about a *guy* here, not a *bunny*.'

'I know. I know. But the computer isn't aware of that, do you see? It simply *reads* its environment and then makes the appropriate adjustments. We'd intended to build as much flexibility into its programme as possible, but this is far better than any of us had hoped.'

Almost despite himself, Blanchard looked impressed. At first he had stared at Jack as if he was a raving lunatic while Jack was telling him the story. But now he seemed convinced.

Niles peered close into Jack's eyes.

'Can you see me, Lieutenant? Good work. A job well done!'

'I can't believe what I'm hearing,' said Tuck's voice from within Jack. 'Find out what went wrong!'

'Why didn't you come to me sooner with this?' Blanchard was asking Niles.

'Lieutenant Pendelton wants to know what went wrong,' Jack said.

'*I'll* tell him what went wrong,' Blanchard said, and then he leaned close to Jack's ear and began to whisper so that Niles couldn't hear him. 'You threw in with a bunch of amateurs, that's what went wrong. These egg-heads don't know squat about security.' Then, speaking louder for Niles's benefit, he went on: 'But don't worry, Tuck old buddy, we're gonna do everything possible to get you out of this civilian.'

'You'd better,' Tuck said vehemently. 'You two-faced sonofabitch!'

Jack flushed with embarrassment. Then he realized that Blanchard couldn't actually hear Tuck.

'Tuck says, thanks,' he announced.

Blanchard smiled. 'Would you excuse us for a moment?' he said to Jack.

'Sure,' Jack replied.

Blanchard went out of the office with Niles. They walked into the lab next door.

'Looks like you're home free now,' Jack said to Tuck.

'Don't count on it,' Tuck replied. 'I've never trusted Pete Blanchard, and I'm not about to start now. Can you see where they went?'

'Yeah,' said Jack, peering through the glass. 'I can see them.'

Blanchard and Niles were already in earnest conversation. Tuck hastily made some adjustments to the dials on his console.

'Look directly at them,' he told Jack. 'Don't turn your head. I think I can beef up this reception a little.'

Jack obeyed. Suddenly Niles's voice was heard from the pod's speaker – blasting at ear-shattering level. Tuck instantly adjusted the volume. The picture on the screen reeled as Jack rocked back.

'What are you doing? What are you doing?' he demanded.

'Don't worry, it's all right now.'

Suddenly Niles could be heard, talking at normal voice-level: '. . . we're not the only ones who have been working with miniaturization, you know . . .'

'Hey!' said a startled Jack. 'I can hear them!'

'I know,' said Tuck. 'Ain't I a clever boy? Now just be quiet for a few minutes. And don't forget to keep looking straight ahead at the two of them.'

'. . . but we're the first,' Niles was continuing, 'to have perfected the trickly re-enlargement process . . . by using *two chips*. One of them is still inside the pod. But the other one's been stolen.'

Blanchard thought it over. 'What do we have to do in order to save Pendelton?'

'Recover the stolen chip. It's as simple – and as difficult – as that.'

'Don't you have duplicates?'

'No. These chips are prototypes. We *can* duplicate them, of course. But not before nine o'clock tomorrow morning.'

Blanchard gave a puzzled frown. 'What's so import-ant about nine o'clock?'

'That's when the pod's air supply runs out.'

Inside Jack, Tuck went cold. He had forgotten, of course. In the original experiment, he was only meant to inhabit the rabbit for a few hours at most. The pod wasn't equipped for a long stay.

'That's no problem,' Blanchard was saying. 'All Pendelton has to do is take his pod into the guy's lungs, open the hatch and grab all the air he needs.'

Tuck grinned with sheer relief. Why hadn't he thought of that himself – it was so simple. But then his hopes were instantly crushed: 'He can't open the hatch,' Niles said. 'The sudden loss of cabin pressure would cause the pod to explode like a balloon.'

Dammit, thought Tuck. Now he really was in trou-ble. Already the air in the pod felt a bit stuffy – or was it just his imagination?

Blanchard looked at his watch, then glanced through the observation window at Jack.

'In that case,' he said softly to Niles, 'we don't really have to do *anything*, do we?'

Niles frowned. 'What do you mean?'

'I mean, the stolen chip's useless without the one inside the pod, isn't it? And we've got that one.'

'So?'

'You go ahead and make your duplicates. It doesn't matter how long it takes. Soon we'll be in business.'

'But what about Pendelton?'

Blanchard shrugged. 'Well, we can't save him, that much is obvious. Perhaps we can use him to bring the perpetrators out into the open.'

Niles looked shocked by Blanchard's cold-hearted pragmatism. Inside the pod, Tuck was furious.

'Do you think he means it?' Jack murmured.

'Of course he means it!' Tuck replied. 'He's talking about using us as *bait*! *Both* of us! Find my jacket!'

'Your what?'

'My *jacket*! It should be here somewhere, in one of the lockers.'

Dutifully Jack went over to the wall against which the lockers were stacked. He began trying the doors, most of which wouldn't open. Then he found one which held a brown leather jacket.

'That's it!' Tuck shouted. 'Okay! The keys are in the pocket –'

'The keys?'

'*Car* keys, Jack! And the car's out back. See the metal door over there? Use it!'

Jack saw the door. He hesitated, the keys in his hand.

'What are you waiting for?!' Tuck wanted to know.

'Don't rush me,' said Jack. 'Just be quiet and let me think this through.'

Tuck could hardly believe it. Did the guy have a proper grasp of the situation? This was no time for hesitation. He controlled himself sufficiently to talk to Jack in as measured a tone as possible:

'Jack, excuse me, but I want you to consider *this*. You heard the guy. My air supply is running out. If you don't help me, you're gonna wind up with a miniaturized submersible pod floating around your insides for good. And inside it is going to be a dead body, slowly rotting away. *Me*, Jack. I'll be *dead*!'

65

Tuck could immediately tell that he had hit the right nerve: Jack was revolted at the thought.

'Okay,' he said. 'But you have to do something for me in return.'

'Anything!' Jack shouted. 'Anything you want. But can we talk about it later? First let's go!'

Jack relented. He hurried off through the metal door. It led down a narrow fire-escape corridor of bare concrete and gave out on to the car park.

'That's the one,' Tuck said. 'The red '69 Mustang Mach I convertible.'

Jack hurried across to the car and climbed in.

The engine fired first time. Jack, under Tuck's urging, gave it full throttle, and they roared away from the lab and turned on to the freeway.

As soon as the lab was out of sight, Jack said, 'I did what you asked.'

'I'm grateful, believe me,' Tuck replied.

'Now I want something in return.'

'Okay. What's the deal?'

'No hurting.'

'Huh?'

'That's what I want from you. *No hurting*.'

'What d'you mean?'

'Don't do anything weird in there. Don't cause an embolism. Or an aneurysm. Or anything else with a funny-sounding name. And stay clear of the brain and the spinal cord – I could end up crippled for life.'

Jack was clutching the steering wheel rigidly with both hands, and it was obvious to Tuck how tense and uptight he was. Tuck found Jack curiously amusing.

'I promise,' he said. 'No hurting. Okay?'

'Okay.'

66

Jack drove on in silence for a while, keeping up his speed and dodging past slower-moving cars.

'What's it like in there, anyway?' he asked.

Tuck peered out through the dome. The searchlights provided two patches of illumination which revealed the glistening, pinkish linings of Jack's innards which had already become almost familiar to Tuck. It was strange how you could get used to the weirdest of things simply because you *had* to.

'It's dark,' Tuck told Jack. 'Like moving through a lot of wet, slimy caverns that throb and pulse – '

'Forget it!' Jack said hastily. 'I'm sorry I asked.'

Tuck saw Jack preparing to overtake a heavy truck.

'Hey!' he cried. 'Watch out! Give that baby plenty of room, will you?'

'Okay, okay,' said Jack. 'I *am* a licensed driver, you know.'

He overtook the truck without difficulty.

'Just don't want the merchandise damaged,' Tuck told him. 'This car's a classic.' Then a note of sad confession entered his voice: 'It's the only thing I own that isn't crap.'

Unseen by both Jack and Tuck, a black Mercedes was on their tail. It kept its distance as Jack turned off the freeway. Following Tuck's instructions, Jack finally pulled up outside Tuck's apartment.

'Wow,' said Jack. 'You've got a great view of the Bay.'

'Never mind the view,' said Tuck. 'Let's get inside.'

On entering the apartment, Jack gazed with dismay at the disorder in the living room. He kept his own place reasonably neat, and this was a mess in comparison.

'Is this where you *live*?' he said, almost as if the matter was in doubt.

'Yeah,' Tuck said defensively. 'What's wrong with it?'

'Oh nothing,' Jack said hastily. 'It looks very comfortable . . .'

'I call it user-friendly,' Tuck said. 'I know where everything is.'

'Amazing,' Jack murmured. He spotted the mechanical arm, picked it up and began to play with it. 'What is this?'

'Never mind,' said Tuck. It felt strange to arrive home in someone else's body. Looking at the place through Jack's eyes somehow made him realize just what a mess it looked to outsiders and he felt a bit ashamed of his slovenly habits.

'I could use a drink right now,' he said. 'What about you?'

'Me?' Jack sounded surprised. 'No thanks.'

'Don't say that. I need a drink, and that means *you* gotta take it for me. That's part of the arrangement.'

He heard Jack sigh. 'Where do you keep it?'

'Look under the sofa cushion,' Tuck told him. 'See if there's a bottle of Cutty Sark there, would ya?'

Obediently Jack checked under the cushion and found the bottle.

'Great!' said Tuck. 'Okay, here's what you do. Just take a nice big tug on that baby and let me do the rest.'

Tuck was already taking the pod right up to the top of Jack's throat. He had emptied the acid from the flask and rinsed it with his water supply. This time he was going to get the liquor *before* it got mixed up with Jack's digestive juices.

He extended one of the pod's mechanical arms, the empty flask grasped between its claws, top off. Tuck peered through the viewing dome, checking that the arm and the flask were properly in place.

'Are you ready?' he said to Jack.

'I'm ready.'

'Okay – down the hatch.'

He saw Jack pausing to wipe the mouth of the bottle with his handkerchief.

'Do I really have to do this?' he asked.

'Come on!' said Tuck. 'I need it!'

'I'm not much of a drinker,' Jack told him, 'but here goes . . .'

Tuck saw the bottle being raised to Jack's lips a second or so before the amber liquid came gushing through the space under his dangling epiglottis. Once again the pod was buffeted by the swirling current, and once again it went plunging down in the dark recesses of Jack's throat, rolling and bumping as it went.

This time, Tuck was ready for the ride. He was firmly strapped into his seat, and had his finger on the claw-retraction controls. He hit the controls immediately, and the arm retracted. By the time the pod came to rest in Jack's stomach, the claw and flask had slid into the pod through the air-lock opening.

Jack eagerly grabbed the flask and sloshed it around under his nose as before. This time, it smelt just right. He threw back a big mouthful, swallowed.

The liquid burned down his throat like napalm, but it was the real thing, unadulterated by any of Jack's gastric juices. Tuck gasped with surprise at the sheer strength of it. He pounded his fist against the edge of the console and made a complete turn in his swivel chair.

Then he took another belt from the flask.

Savouring the second mouthful, Tuck looked up at the monitor. Jack was studying the label of the bottle and saying, 'Hey, this stuff's not bad. It relaxes you.'

Then *he* took another swig.

Tuck sat with his feet up on the console of the pod, tapping his toes together and taking shots of whisky from the flask as Sam Cooke sang 'Twistin' the Night Away'. He had brought a selection of his favourite tapes aboard the pod, and 'Sam Cooke's Greatest Hits' was perhaps his favourite of all. The liquor had had the desired effect: he felt mellow, at peace with himself.

Jack, too, was also having fun. The music was playing in his head as if he had a pair of ear-phones on, and he was singing along and actually twisting around Tuck's apartment, weaving occasionally to avoid the bits of motorcycle that lay on the floor. The bottle of Cutty Sark was empty.

'I never knew that dancing could be this much fun,' he remarked.

'Try it with a girl some time,' Tuck said to him.

Jack dodged an exhaust pipe and spotted a framed photograph of an attractive fair-haired woman on the table.

'Someone like this maybe,' he said, picking the photograph up and peering at it.

Tuck, suddenly confronted with Lydia's face, felt a deep pang of regret. He had not seen or heard from Lydia since she had walked out of the apartment a month ago.

'Yeah,' he said. 'Somebody like that.'

'Who is she?' Jack asked.

'Her name's Lydia Maxwell. She's a reporter.'

'You two going out together?'

'That's *my* business,' Tuck said firmly. 'I may be stuck in your body, but that doesn't mean I'm going to tell you all the details of my private life.'

Jack didn't pursue the subject. He flopped on to the sofa, feeling pleasantly calm and philosophical for once.

'It's incredible, isn't it?' he remarked. 'You're seeing parts of my body I'll *never* get to see.'

'Believe me,' Tuck said, 'you aren't missing much.'

'The gastric mucosa,' Jack went on, as if he hadn't heard him, 'intestinal villi, pulmonary alveoli.' Jack stifled a burp. 'Far-away places with strange sounding names.'

Tuck began to wonder about Jack. For an ordinary guy like him to know such medical terms must mean that he had a fascination with the workings of the human body. And from what he already knew of Jack, it was a *morbid* fascination.

'Jack,' he said. 'Go look in the mirror for me, will you?'

Jack was still wrapped in wonder at the idea of Tuck being shrunken inside him.

'What?' he said. 'Why?'

'Because I just realized I don't know what you look like,' Tuck said. 'I mean, from the *outside*.'

With some difficulty, Jack managed to raise himself up from the sofa. The room seemed to wobble around him. He managed to stagger over to the mirror on the wall and peer into it blearily.

71

Tuck took one look at his face and he knew they were in trouble. Even relaxed by the whisky, he looked harrassed and hyper-sensitive.

'You know what?' he said. 'We're gonna need more help.'

'What d'you mean?' asked Jack.

'Can you drive?'

'Of course I can drive. You saw me doing it earlier.'

'No – I mean, are you fit to drive? Are you sober enough?'

'Sure I am,' Jack said brazenly. He took a step forward as if to prove to Jack that he could walk in a straight line, but the step swiftly turned into a stagger, and he almost collapsed on to the sofa.

'Make some coffee,' Tuck said urgently. 'Make it quick and make it *very, very* strong.'

7

Lydia Maxwell sat on the corner of her desk in the press room, conferring with her editor, Harry Paxton. Harry leaned back in his chair, a sceptical expression on his face.

'"Espionage in Silicon Valley,"' he quoted. '"The Buying and Selling of Advanced Technology".' He sucked on his teeth. 'It sounded like Sunday Supplement stuff to me *then*, and that's how it sounds to me now. I know you've been on the tail of this story for weeks, Lydia, but I've still got nothing concrete. Maybe we'll have to wait until people start getting murdered. Then we might be able to print something.'

'People *are* getting murdered,' Lydia was quick to reply. 'A scientist named Ozzie Wexler – he was gunned down this morning in a shopping mall. Nobody saw who did it.'

Harry sat up in his chair, at last beginning to take her seriously. 'What do you know about this guy Wexler?'

'A bit more than the police. I've been doing some checking. He worked for a lab called Vectorscope. It's located near the mall.

'Something got stolen, maybe?' said a third voice.

It was Duane Flornoy, a close colleague of Lydia's. He leaned across the desk.

'I don't know Duane,' Lydia said. 'Vectorscope's

buttoned up as tight as a drum, and I haven't been able to get anything out of them. Why do you ask?'

Flornoy made a movement of someone drawing imaginary guns from belt holsters.

'*The Cowboy*,' he said dramatically.

Lydia peered at him, wide-eyed. 'Is he in town?'

'The Cowboy?' said Harry. 'Who's he?'

'He's on his way right now,' Flornoy told Lydia. He glanced at the notepad which he had put down on the desk. 'TWA flight 607, arriving San Francisco International five o'clock this afternoon. I checked.'

'Who the hell is this guy?' Harry insisted.

Lydia was intrigued. 'He's a fence,' she told her editor. 'He works out of the Middle East, but he likes to dress Wild West style. He specializes in trips to the States, buying the latest technology from anyone who'll sell and then taking it back to his masters at home. Nobody's really sure who he works for, only that they're not a very pleasant lot. He's tough. *Very*, *very* tough. I've heard some amazing stories about him.'

'You make him sound like Superman,' Harry remarked.

Lydia tapped a pencil thoughtfully against her lips.

'That may not be so far from the mark,' she observed.

The pilot of the aircraft had already begun his descent, and the stewardess moved purposefully down the central corridor, checking that everyone was securely belted in. Then she spotted clouds of blue smoke coming from a seat at the rear of the plane. She hastened forward.

A big, swarthy man was sitting there, dressed in a

white felt Stetson hat, a suede Western sports coat over a bib-front shirt and blue jeans tucked into fancy snakeskin cowboy boots. He was reading a foreign edition of *People* magazine while puffing on a fat cigar. The mild-mannered man sitting next to him was unsuccessfully trying to fan the smoke away from his face.

The stewardess knelt beside the man, giving him her best professional smile.

'I'm sorry, sir,' she said. 'We've already begun our descent.'

'So?'

The word came out blunt and thickly accented. The stewardess broadened her smile and said, 'You'll have to extinguish your cigar.'

For a moment the man did nothing. For a moment the stewardess entertained the horrible thought that he was going to stub it in her face. Then a smile broke out on his rugged features. It was not a pleasant smile, more a grimace.

Then, to her amazement, he crushed out the cigar in the palm of his hand, without flinching, without a flicker of change in his expression.

Jack was approaching the newspaper offices in the car when Tuck spotted Lydia emerging from the main entrance.

'There she is!' he called.

'Where?' said Jack.

Lydia had already been swallowed up by the crowd on the sidewalk. She looked as if she was in a big hurry.

'She just came out of the building,' Tuck said. 'Quick! She's getting away. Honk the horn!'

75

Jack obliged. The horn made a tootling noise quite unlike any he had ever heard before. The sound was so distinctive that Jack wasn't surprised to see Lydia emerge from the crowd. He recognized her immediately from her photograph. The sun shone gold on her hair and her eyes were bright.

Jack had pulled the Mustang over to the kerb, and he hastily wound down the window as Lydia approached. She looked gorgeous, and when she leant into the car he could smell an expensive perfume that made him want to throw his arms around her. But she was frowning.

'I *know* this car,' she said to him. 'This car belongs to Tuck Pendelton.'

Jack nodded like a broken-backed doll. 'Right,' he managed to say.

'So what are you doing driving it?' she wanted to know. 'Tuck would sooner trust somebody with his *life* than with his car.'

Jack tried to say something, but he didn't know how to begin.

'Who are you anyway?' Lydia demanded. 'Does Tuck know you have his – hey, isn't that Tuck's jacket? That *is* Tuck's jacket. You're wearing his jacket!'

Jack had put the jacket on before leaving the apartment. More than ever, he didn't know what to say.

'Lydia!' shouted Tuck from inside him. 'Shut up and listen!'

Automatically, Jack passed the message on: 'Lydia! Shut up and listen!'

She gave him a very curious stare. 'How do you know my name?'

'Tuck told me,' Jack managed to say. 'I'm a friend of his.'

She continued staring, still looking doubtful.

'Tell her you have to talk to her,' Tuck said.

'I have to talk to you,' Tuck parroted aloud.

'So talk,' she said.

'Somewhere quiet!' Tuck said earnestly. 'Suggest a restaurant or something. Tell her I'm in trouble.'

'Tuck's in trouble,' Jack said. 'Can we go somewhere private to talk?'

Still she was suspicious. She considered, then said, 'All right. If Tuck is really in trouble . . . But I warn you, if you try anything funny – I'm a black belt in karate!'

'She's lying,' Tuck whispered.

But Jack was too busy gazing longingly at Lydia to listen.

Ten minutes later, Jack and Lydia were sitting opposite one another at a quiet restaurant table, each with a cup of coffee in front of them.

'So what sort of trouble is Tuck in?' Lydia wanted to know.

Jack suddenly went blank. How could he possibly tell her the truth?

'Say I've been kidnapped,' Tuck told him. 'Tell her I'm being held to ransom.'

Jack repeated this to Lydia. She raised her eyebrows in surprise.

'Tuck's being held to ransom?'

'In a manner of speaking, yes.'

'Why?'

With Tuck prompting him, Jack said, 'We need a

certain microchip to get him back. It was taken from the Vectorscope lab this morning.'

'So there *was* a break-in!' Lydia said triumphantly. 'I thought as much. And I had a hunch that Tuck was involved with Vectorscope. But how? And what's *your* involvement?'

She was scrutinizing him doubtfully, and Jack was pretty sure that he didn't pass muster as a scientist-type.

'Me?' he said. 'Well, that's a long story.'

'Good,' said Lydia. 'I'm a reporter. I *like* long stories.'

Once again, Jack was at a loss. He took a gulp of his coffee.

'Jack,' said Tuck, 'don't let her take control of the conversation! She's a woman – dominate her! Be aggressive! Be *me*!'

The idea of dominating anyone was foreign to Jack's nature, but he knew he had to try to take control. He drew himself up, tried to look as tough and as steadfast as he could.

'Look, Lydia – you'll just have to trust me, okay? There's no time for explanations. We only have until nine o'clock tomorrow morning. Now I understand you have some knowledge of corporate espionage.'

Tuck had filled him in on something of Lydia's background as a reporter. But Lydia was looking anxious.

'Nine o'clock?' she said. 'What happens then?'

'That's when Tuck . . . uh, the deadline, expires.'

'Can't we negotiate for more time?'

'Uh . . . no . . . we can't.'

'Why not? Where is he, anyway? Where do they have him?'

'Where? . . .' Again Jack was becoming flustered, his attempt to take charge already crumbling away.

'He's close by,' he said hastily. 'In the area. Somewhere in the immediate vicinity. It's hard to say exactly.'

'Who has him?'

Her blue eyes were so penetrating and direct. 'Who?' said Jack.

'Yes. *Who?*'

Jack surged to his feet. 'Would you excuse me a minute?' Then he bolted for the men's room.

Outside, a black Mercedes had parked in one of the spaces reserved for disabled drivers. A traffic cop was walking around the car, looking distinctly displeased. But there was no sign of its driver.

Jack stood in front of the urinal. Another restaurant customer was washing his hands at the sink.

'I blew it,' Jack said to Tuck. 'I can't handle her.'

'You didn't do so bad,' Tuck told him. 'She's a tough cookie.'

'She's a *beautiful* tough cookie,' Jack said.

The customer at the sink glanced across at him.

'What's that got to do with anything?' Tuck was saying.

'Nothing,' Jack replied. 'But I can't keep this up. We should tell her the truth.'

The customer continued staring, watching Jack looking down at the urinal, apparently talking to himself.

'Absolutely not!' Tuck was saying. 'She wouldn't believe it.' He paused. 'Besides, it's humiliating being this small. There – I've said it.'

79

'What's so bad about being small?' Jack wanted to know.

He dried his hands and went out into the restaurant, not noticing Igoe, who was sitting at a small table in a corner, peering over the top of his menu.

But Lydia saw Igoe rise as Jack went past, and all her instincts told her that something was wrong. At that moment, Igoe made his move, grabbing Jack by the arm.

Jack, on seeing who it was, immediately panicked and began trying to wrench his arm free. Lydia rose, pulling from her shoulder-purse something that resembled a gun.

'Hold it!' she shouted across the restaurant.

The other patrons looked up, and several of them began to scream and take cover under their tables. Igoe froze, still holding Jack's arm.

'This is an electronic stun-gun,' Lydia told him. 'A non-lethal personal defence weapon deploying a charge of 20,000 volts. It will immobilize you for up to fifteen minutes and probably render you unconscious as well. So just let go of that man!' She turned to a startled waiter: 'Call the police!'

Igoe whipped Jack towards him. Instinctively Lydia squeezed the trigger.

A stun-dart shot from the weapon. It hit Jack straight in the right breast.

'No!' Lydia shouted.

The dart penetrated Jack's plastic name-tag, melting it instantly. Half the charge was released with a loud buzz. The other half entered Jack's body. He felt a jolt like a strong electric shock, and went limp in Igoe's arms.

Inside Jack, Tuck also felt the impact of the electrical charge. Crackling white ribbons of electric current danced around the contours of the pod, lighting the interior of Jack's body with an unearthly glow. Tuck was slammed back into his seat as he, too, succumbed to the stunning effect of the electric charge.

Igoe did not hesitate. He grabbed Jack's limp body and slung it over his shoulder like a sack of flour. Something tinkled on to the floor, but Igoe didn't notice. Inside Jack, Tuck was turned upside-down. Igoe ran off, bursting out through the restaurant doors before Lydia or the startled customers could do anything further.

The whole place was filled with yelling and screaming.

'Someone call the police!' Lydia shouted.

She darted over and plucked from the floor the keys which had fallen from Jack's pocket when he was slung over Igoe's shoulder. Lydia instantly recognized them as the keys to Tuck's Mustang.

Igoe emerged with Jack at the very instant that his Mercedes was being towed away by a police truck. He gave an animal-like growl of frustration, then peered around him. A delivery truck was pulling away from a loading dock nearby. Carrying Jack as if he weighed no more than a bag of shopping, Igoe darted over, wrenched the truck's doors open and bundled Jack inside.

He slammed the doors as the truck began to pick up speed. Igoe ran alongside it, leapt up on to the running board and threw open the cab door. Before the startled driver could do anything, he yanked him out, flinging him to the ground, and jumped into the driver's seat, taking over the wheel.

Lydia saw the truck pull away with Igoe driving. She ran for the Mustang.

Tuck returned to consciousness. Everything was dark. It took him a few moments to remember where he was. He began fumbling around, found the instrument panel, then pressed the emergency power button.

The console blinked to life again. Tuck was still lying upside down in the pod, but with the engines working he was quickly able to right it.

The screen which should have been showing the scene through Jack's eyes remained blank.

'Jack! Jack!' Tuck shouted. 'Are you all right? What happened? Seems like we experienced a massive power surge.'

There was no response from Jack. Concerned, Tuck studied the instruments which gave readings of Jack's vital functions. One of the gauges gave him immediate cause for alarm.

'What's going on, Jack?! Your heart rate's slowing way down. Jack! Jack!'

'Ummgghh . . .'

'Jack? Is that you? It has to be! Dammit, Jack, wake up!'

The screen colour altered slightly, still remaining dark. Tuck was certain that Jack had opened his eyes, but there was nothing to be seen.

'I'm f-f-f-f-f-f-' Jack began.

'Jack!' Tuck said with relief. 'You had me worried there. Thought I'd lost you for a minute, kid.'

There was no reply from Jack.

82

'What happened?' Tuck asked. 'Where's Lydia? Where are *we*? I can't see a thing. Why's it so dark?'

'I'm f-f-f-f-f-f-' Jack started again.

'You're *what*? Can't make you out, Jack. Message garbled. Try again.'

'I'm f-f-f-f-f-*freezing*!'

'You're freezing?'

'We must be in the back of a delivery truck,' Jack told him. 'It's refrigerated.'

'What's that tapping sound?'

'That's my teeth chattering!'

8

Lydia turned the Mustang off the secluded stretch of road and parked it out of sight. Then she crept up to the top of a low rise and peered over.

The truck had BERMAN'S FROZEN FOOD SUPPLY CO. on its side. A limousine had pulled up beside it, and a white-haired man in a five-hundred-dollar suit climbed out. Meanwhile the big guy Lydia had shot at in the restaurant was flinging open the back doors of the truck. He hauled out Jack, whose entire body was covered with a thin layer of white frost. Behind them rose the Golden Gate Bridge, traffic continuing to stream across it, unaware of the little drama being enacted below. Lydia crept forward, trying to get within earshot of the group.

The white-haired man was tall, and he looked quite ruthless and power-crazy. One of his henchmen tossed a fur-coat over the shoulders of Jack, who stood there, blinking at him, his eyelashes coated with snowflakes. Lydia felt a pang of almost maternal sympathy for him.

'The name is Scrimshaw,' the white-haired man said to Jack. 'Victor Scrimshaw. It's quite a pleasure to make your acquaintance.'

But he made it sound more like a threat than a pleasure, and he did not offer his hand.

'Dr Canker!' he shouted. 'Come out here!'

An attractive woman climbed out of the limousine and walked over to Jack. She produced a stethoscope

from the pocket of her expensive overcoat and proceeded to check Jack's quivering chest.

'Well?' Scrimshaw said impatiently.

'Hypothermia,' Canker announced. 'Quite mild.'

'Will he live?'

'Oh, yes. *If* you want him to.'

Scrimshaw appeared to mull it over. 'Do we need
him alive?' he asked.

'Oh, yes,' Canker said. 'It would be preferable.'

Lydia saw Jack almost collapse with relief.

Scrimshaw turned to the henchman. 'Bring some
blankets from the car.'

Canker, still scrutinizing Jack, began to smile.

'I know how to warm him up,' she said, and she ran
her hands down Jack's body. Jack began to quiver even
more strongly.

'Knock it off, Margaret!' Scrimshaw ordered. 'Here
come the blankets.'

The henchman proceeded to drape them over Jack
until only his head was visible above a pyramid of red
tartan.

'Time we were going,' Scrimshaw announced. 'Put
him back in the truck. *I'll* accompany him. Jack, isn't
it?' He patted Jack on the back, and a small shower of
frost fell around his feet. 'We're going to have a little
chat, Jack.'

'Let *me* sit with him,' Canker pleaded.

'Forget it, Margaret. You take the limo.'

Jack was still frozen under the mound of blankets.
Scrimshaw sat beside him, wreathed in a big fur coat,
puffing on a thick cigar. His manner was very chummy
in a perfectly menacing way.

'Nuclear weapons, Jack,' he said. 'They mean nothing. Everybody's got 'em, but nobody's got the guts to use 'em. Am I right or am I right?'

Jasck had begun to shiver again. He eyed Scrimshaw warily, saying nothing.

'What about *space*,' Scrimshaw went on.

'I've got plenty of room,' Jack managed to say.

'Not *that* kind of space, Jack – *outer* space. It's a flop – did you know that? Not many people do. It's just an endless junk yard of orbiting debris.' He spat a fragment of tobacco from his mouth. 'Ahhh . . . but *miniaturization,* Jack. *That's* the ticket. That's the coming thing, you know. It's the edge everyone's been looking for. But *who* will have that edge, Jack? What country will control miniaturization?'

Jack considered the question. It was a very complex one, and he had no idea of the answer.

'Frankly,' Scrimshaw said, 'I don't give a damn. I'm only in this for the money.' He paused, smiling again. 'And *that's* why we gotta get that little pod out from inside you.'

So saying, he jabbed Jack in the ribs with his finger. Even through the mound of blankets, Jack felt it, and he realized that he was finally beginning to warm up. But the idea of Scrimshaw extracting the pod from his body was the stuff of which his worst nightmares were made.

Scrimshaw settled back to enjoy his cigar. Jack began to squirm in the bucket seat in which he was perched.

'Jack,' said Tuck's voice from within him, 'there's nobody more dangerous than the man who's only in it for the money.'

'You don't have to tell me!' Jack said emphatically.

86

'What was that?' Scrimshaw asked.

'Nothing,' Jack assured him. 'Just thinking aloud.'

Scrimshaw did not press him. Huddled under the blankets, Jack now felt much warmer.

'Glance around slowly,' said Tuck, 'so that I can get the lay of the land.'

It was no longer pitch-black in the back of the truck, Jack belatedly realized. He peered around at the boxes of food, the hulking fur-coated Scrimshaw, and finally at the truck's doors . . .

A crack of light showed through them.

'The doors aren't properly closed, Jack!' Tuck yelled. 'The latch isn't in place.'

Jack kept silent. His eyes were watering from the noxious fumes of Scrimshaw's cigars, but at least he no longer felt as if he was freezing to death.

'Jack,' Tuck said urgently, 'this is it. The doors are unlocked. We can take them by surprise – bust outta here before they know what's hit them!'

Jack stared at the doors. He did not move or speak.

'Can you do it?' asked Tuck. 'Cough if you can.'

Jack's heart had begun to palpitate at the prospect. He knew only too well that he was the Clark Kent rather than the Superman type. He kept quiet.

'Okay, Jack,' said Tuck. 'Listen to me. This is your moment. It's all come down to this. Remember the phoney messenger with the gun, Jack? Remember how you handled him? You found the strength, Jack. You found the nerve. You reached down inside yourself and you found it. And *I* was right there with you, Jack – and I'll be right here with you again. You can do it.'

Jack began to nibble on his lip. Still he remained silent.

'Jack,' Tuck urged him, 'you're not the same man you were this morning. You're better. You're stronger. You're in control of your own destiny.'

I'm terrified! Jack thought. But as he sat there, listening to Tuck's prompting, he began to feel that he *had* to do something to try to escape. For too long he'd let people push him around, let his life be determined by the whims and demands of others. Without courage, without determination, he was never going to achieve anything worthwhile.

'Psyche yourself up,' Tuck was telling him. 'Psyche yourself up. Look at the doors again.'

Jack looked.

'You're not gonna stack soup cans all your life, are you, Jack? See yourself leaping to your feet, making a bid for freedom. You're not going to bag groceries until you die, are you, Jack? See yourself pushing open the doors! See yourself jumping from the truck! See yourself being a hero, Jack! Can you see it! *Can you see it*!'

'I can see it!' Jack yelled, flinging off all his blankets and jumping to his feet.

'Eh?' said Scrimshaw, totally surprised and bewildered.

Jack leapt forward.

'Jack!' Tuck shouted. 'No! Wait until – '

But Jack wasn't listening. He charged towards the truck's doors and flung them open.

' – the truck has stopped!' Tuck finished.

But it was too late. The doors swung out as Jack barged them, the highway flying by underneath at sixty miles an hour.

'Ohhhhhhhhhh!' said Jack, clinging on to one of the doors with all his might as it swung right open.

Scrimshaw lurched to his feet and stumbled forward. He reached out through the open back end and tried to make a grab for Jack, but Jack swung out of his reach.

The jolting movement of the truck caused Jack to flap back and forth as he clung on to the door. Several times Scrimshaw tried to grab him, but every time Jack swung away again at the last second.

Jack was frozen with terror, clinging on for dear life. Then he noticed Tuck's Mustang on the tail of the truck. Lydia was driving. She was some distance back, but quickly she began to close the gap.

Inside the truck, Scrimshaw went to the front and began to pound on the back wall of the driver's cab. Igoe was at the wheel. He did not look around. Scrimshaw could hear classical music blasting out from the cab – Wagner's 'Entrance of the Gods into Valhalla'. It was coming full volume out of the radio. Scrimshaw pounded again, but Igoe remained completely unaware of him.

The door on which Jack was hanging began to swing back in again. Scrimshaw darted forward, then slipped on the icy floor and sat down heavily.

On seeing this, Jack gave a maniacal laugh as the door swung out again. Scrimshaw glared furiously at him, clambering to his feet. The door started to swing inwards once more.

Grinning evilly, Scrimshaw reached out two claw-like hands to grab Jack. But at the last moment, Jack lashed out with his foot, kicking him in the chest and sending him careening backward into a pile of frozen fish cartons.

As the door lurched outwards again, Jack heard Lydia shouting: 'Jump, Jack! Jump into the car!'

He peered down and saw the Mustang directly below him. He did nothing.

'Jump!' Lydia urged him. 'Jump!'

He shook his head at her. Then he saw Scrimshaw climbing to his feet, brushing off boxes of frozen fish, then starting murderously towards him.

He let his feet drop down into the Mustang but continued clinging on to the door with his hands. At that moment the two vehicles began to drift apart. Jack felt like a stretching rubber band, his hands attached to the truck, his feet tucked under the headrest of the seat next to Lydia's. Fearful that he was going to be torn apart, he kicked his feet free.

Lydia instantly reached out and grabbed the leg of his trousers.

'Let go!' she shouted to him.

'Let go?' he screamed back. 'Are you *crazy*!'

Jack was fully stretched. Just as he thought he was going to split in half, Lydia managed to steer the Mustang closer to the truck once more.

'*Now* let go!' she shouted.

Jack didn't want to. But the door was beginning to swing back in again, and Scrimshaw looked like a demon, hell-bent on tearing him apart with his bare hands. Jack loosened his grip, and he fell backwards into the Mustang's passenger seat. Lydia immediately took her foot off the gas, and the truck surged away, speeding ahead.

There was a slip-road up ahead. She swung on the wheel, turning the car off the freeway. Jack lay like a shipwrecked man in the seat beside her. Deep within him, Tuck, who had witnessed most of the action, reached for his flask to take a shot of Cutty Sark. Then he thought better of it and put the flask away. He *had* to stay sober if they were going to have any chance of recovering the second microchip.

Meanwhile the frozen food van was still hurtling along the freeway, the doors banging open and shut. Scrimshaw resumed his pounding on the back of the driver's cab, his face going red with frustration and fury.

'Igoe!' he screamed. 'Igoe! Stop the goddamned truck!'

Wagner continued blaring from the radio, and Igoe kept staring straight ahead, his one good hand gripped tightly around the wheel.

The banging of the doors was giving Scrimshaw a headache. He managed to grab them, wrench them shut. Then he went back and continued hammering his fists at the cab.

Suddenly the music ended.

'Igoe!' Scrimshaw yelled. 'You blockheaded oaf!'

Igoe finally turned his head, peering through the tiny window.

'Turn the goddamned truck off the road!' Scrimshaw shouted at the top of his voice.

At last Igoe obliged, bumping the truck over a stretch of scrubby ground until they were out of sight of all the other vehicles on the freeway.

Scrimshaw flung open the back doors and jumped down. The air felt positively tropical after the chill of the refrigerated container. Steam began to rise from his fur coat.

Igoe climbed out of the cab and walked around to

him, frowning with puzzlement. Scrimshaw simply stood there, saying nothing, waiting until he looked into the back of the truck.

Igoe stared at the empty bucket seat, at the scattered cartons of frozen food. His frown deepened. Then he leapt up into the back and began rooting around like a big animal searching for its prey. He scattered the cartons around, but found nothing. Finally he peeked out at Scrimshaw.

'Yes,' Scrimshaw said. 'He's gone.'

Scrimshaw was about to vent his fury on Igoe, there being no one else to hand. He would wound him with bitter sarcasm, sting him with irony, make him feel small and stupid. But Igoe pushed back the sleeve of his artificial arm and inserted a magazine clip from his pocket into the automatic rifle attachment there. And, like an enraged beast, he unleashed a fusillade of gunfire at the bucket seat, not stopping until it was cut to pieces.

Scrimshaw swallowed.

'Precisely,' he said to Igoe.

9

The Mustang was parked across the street from the Mark Hopkins Hotel in central San Francisco. Lydia and Jack were sitting inside it, Jack only just recovered from his ordeal.

'What are we doing here?' he asked Lydia.

'Waiting for someone,' she told him.

'Oh.' He liked the way her lips moved when she spoke. In fact, he liked pretty much everything about her. Not only was she beautiful but also brave and resourceful. He stole a glance down at her shapely legs.

'Hey!' Tuck shouted from within. 'Knock it off!'

Jack felt himself blushing.

'What's up?' Lydia asked.

'Nothing,' he said hastily. 'Uh . . . *who* are we waiting for exactly?'

'A man called the Cowboy,' she told him. 'I've been tracking his movements for months. He arrived at the airport an hour ago, and this is where he always stays when he's in town.' She indicated the hotel. 'I have a feeling that he's going to lead us right to that microchip we need.'

Jack frowned. 'Why do you think that?'

'Because he's a fence. He deals in stolen technology – *Western* technology almost exclusively – which he then sells overseas to the highest bidder. Who do you think introduced velcro to the Persian Gulf?'

Jack gazed at her with outright admiration. What an incredible person she was.

'You really like your job, don't you?' he said.

'Some days more than others,' she replied.

Jack peered out the window, suddenly feeling rather morose.

'I hate my job,' he said. 'I've only just realized that.'

'What do you do?'

'I work in a supermarket. I'm the assistant manager. I'm told I have a big future in retail food sales.'

'That's good, isn't it?' Lydia said sympathetically.

'No. It makes me want to slit my wrists.'

Any further discussion of the subject was halted as a cab pulled up to the entrance of the hotel and the Cowboy climbed out.

'It's him!' Lydia said. 'Perfect timing.' She turned to Jack. 'Get the suitcase from the trunk.'

'Why?' Jack asked.

'We're checking into the hotel. It's less suspicious if we have a suitcase.'

They both climbed out of the Mustang and Jack opened the trunk. Sure enough, there was a suitcase inside.

'How did you know it was there?' he asked Lydia.

'Tuck always keeps a packed suitcase in the trunk – just in case he wakes up in a 'strange place' after a night on the booze.'

'Hey,' Tuck said to Jack, 'she's blackening my name.' But there was something in his voice which made Jack realize that Tuck had taken her words to heart.

'I didn't know she knew about the suitcase,' Tuck added, somewhat dolefully.

Ten minutes later, Jack and Lydia had booked into a room at the hotel. Country-and-western music filtered through the wall from next door – the Cowboy was their immediate neighbour. Jack had stolen a look at the hotel book while Lydia kept the receptionist occupied, and then they had asked for the room immediately next door, pretending that they were a married couple and that the room had a sentimental value to them.

'We'll wait here until we hear him leaving,' Lydia said. 'Then we'll follow him.'

'I don't like this married couple bit,' Tuck murmured irritably within Jack.

'What if he just stays in?' Jack said to Lydia.

'He won't. This guy never sleeps. He likes a club called the Inferno. He'll be going there tonight, unless I'm very much mistaken. And we'll be stepping out there, too.'

Jack had never been in a proper club in all his life. The prospect of going with Lydia filled him with pleasure.

'That guy in the truck,' she said to him. 'You said his name was Scrimshaw, right?'

Jack nodded. 'Victor Scrimshaw. He gave me the creeps.'

'I'll check him out,' Lydia said, and she reached for the phone.

Jack watched her, admiring every inch of her.

'I told you to cut that out!' Tuck shouted. 'What are you looking at? I thought you were supposed to be a gentleman.'

Jack stepped back until he was sure he was out of Lydia's earshot.

95

'C'mon, Tuck,' he said. 'Who can blame me? And we're on our second honeymoon after all . . .'

'Forget it! You're not going to be doing any honeymooning with her – '

'Don't you think she has the cutest little over-bite? Gives her mouth this adorable, pouty expression that – '

'I know what she looks like!'

Jack grinned, enjoying the feeling that for once *he* was the person doing the baiting. But at the same time it wasn't entirely a joke as far as he was concerned.

'What's the deal between you two, anyway?'

'Never you mind!'

Lydia was busy talking into the phone. Jack had laid Tuck's suitcase on the bed, and now he unlocked it and flipped open the top. Tuck's clothes were arranged inside. They looked far more stylish than the kind of things Jack normally wore.

'Uh . . . Tuck,' he said, 'I sure could use a change of clothes. Mind if I dip into this suitcase a little?'

'No, no,' Tuck said peevishly. '"Dip" all you like. But nothing will fit you – I'm bigger-built than you.'

Margaret Canker emerged from the bathroom wearing a thin black lace robe. The telephone started ringing, and she picked it up.

'Margaret? Is that you?'

'Yes, it's me, Victor. How is everything?'

'Terrible!' Scrimshaw said. 'The Cowboy's in town, and I still don't have that other chip.'

'Igoe told me what happened. It all sounds rather unfortunate, Victor.'

'Unfortunate! Unfortunate! It was positively disastrous. And it was all Igoe's fault, Margaret. If he had stopped the goddamned truck in time, we could have gone after them and got Jack Putter back.'

At that point Igoe entered the bedroom, wearing a brown silk robe and carrying a bottle of wine and two glasses.

'He's no damned good, Margaret,' Scrimshaw was saying.

Igoe had slipped off his prosthetic arm and replaced it with an electronic corkscrew. He used this to pop the cork on the wine bottle in a matter of seconds. Canker gazed at him with adoration.

'You're crazy, Victor,' she said into the phone. 'He's the most perfect creature on earth!'

'Just get me that chip!' Scrimshaw said angrily, and the line went dead.

'This is one mean dude, Lydia,' Duane Flornoy was saying into the phone. 'I can't believe this guy. He's a lawyer, and he's represented several organized crime figures. He's also been administrator of funds for various black market operations, and he's suspected of secret arms dealing. Yet somehow he manages to keep his nose clean.'

Lydia, perched on the bed in the hotel room, made notes on her pad.

'Anything else?' she asked.

'Yeah. It's odds on he led the raid on Vectorscope.'

Lydia thanked Duane and rang off. When she turned around, she saw Jack dressed in Tuck's shirt and pants with the new jacket she had bought him for his last birthday. Everything was slightly too big, but this only served to make Jack look more fashionable.

She stood up, staring at him wistfully. Then she approached him and ran her hands down the arms of the coat.

'What's the matter?' Jack said somewhat nervously.

'The clothes suit you,' she said. 'You remind me of Tuck in them.'

'Hey – !' Tuck said from within Jack. Suddenly he began to remember the night they had first met. She had been writing the article about him, and afterwards they'd gone out to dinner together. That was the start of the romance. It had been a rocky road since then, with plenty of ups and downs. And most of the downs, he had to admit, had been caused by his drinking. God, he missed her now! He wanted to take her in his arms, crush her against him. Fat chance, when he was no bigger than a bacterium.

'It sounds to me,' Jack was remarking to Lydia, 'as if you're pretty hung up on the guy.'

She went over to the window and peered out, her back to him. 'How well do you know Tuck?'

'We're *very* close,' Jack told her.

'Does he talk about me?'

'He's pretty tight-lipped when it comes to women.'

'Hey!' Tuck shouted, 'Will you knock this off!'

But Jack ignored him. He walked over and stood next to Lydia.

'If *I* were Tuck,' he said, 'I'd talk about you all the time.'

Lydia, peering down into the street, suddenly looked alarmed.

'He's sneaked out!' she said.

'Who?'

98

'The Cowboy. He's leaving. C'mon, let's get after him!'

Hurriedly they went out, taking the emergency stairs down to the parking lot. Jack climbed into the driver's seat of the Mustang with Lydia beside him. As they pulled out, they saw the Cowboy getting into a taxi.

'Keep on his tail!' Lydia whispered.

Jack hung back until the cab pulled away. Then he drew out on to the freeway, following it at a discreet distance.

Beside him, Lydia began to undergo an amazing wardrobe transformation. She was dressed in smart working woman's clothes, a dark shirt and matching jacket over a white blouse with a scarlet scarf tied at her neck. She took the scarf off and belted it around her waist before undoing the top button of her blouse and turning up the collar. By these simple changes she turned from being a career woman into someone who was ready for a stylish night out.

'Wow,' said Jack appreciatively.

Lydia winked at Jack and said, 'I always like to be ready for a quick change operation when necessary. In my job, you never know where you might end up from one hour to the next, and it pays to be prepared.'

Fifteen minutes later the cab pulled up outside the Inferno. It was built of graffiti-scrawled brick, the sign in crimson neon above the entrance. Outside milled a crowd which seemed to comprise an equal mixture of hardcore punks and adventurous yuppies.

As Jack and Lydia climbed out of the Mustang, Jack heard his name being called.

He looked around and saw Wendy approaching. For a second, he didn't recognize her. Her hair was lacquered into spikes and spray-dyed pink and orange. She wore a black leather mini-dress studded with metal spikes and heavy make-up in which deep shades of blue and purple predominated.

She looked equally surprised to see him. She glanced at Lydia, then back at him.

'Jack?' she said. 'Jack?'

She came forward and started stroking him as if she couldn't believe he was real.

'My God, Jack! Look at you!'

Jack peered down at himself. 'Uh . . . what's the matter with me?'

'Nothing. You look great!'

She grinned at him and popped a big pink bubble of gum.

Jack didn't know quite what to say. Wendy looked nothing like the girl who worked at the supermarket.

'Look at *you*,' he said to her.

Lydia was watching the Cowboy entering the club.

'I'm going in before we lose him!' she said.

Jack made to follow, but Wendy had grabbed his arm, refusing to let him go.

Much later, in the crowded, smoke-filled room, Jack and Wendy danced together as the speakers blasted out a raucous version of some punk anthem. Jack wasn't sure about the music, but he had to admit that he was enjoying himself.

'I can't believe it, Jack,' Wendy was saying. 'It's so exciting! I mean, how long have you been leading this double life?'

Jack merely gave her a knowing smile as if to indicate that he preferred to remain a man of mystery in her eyes. He glanced through the crowd and spotted the

Cowboy dancing wildly at the centre of the floor. Then a figure came weaving through the crowd and shimmied up to him.

It was Lydia, and the Cowboy obviously liked what he saw.

The crowd swallowed them up, and Wendy grabbed hold of him as a particularly vigorous and loud track began to blare out from the speakers.

Some time later, Wendy dragged him off the floor, hot and sweaty, for a drink. When he got back from the bar with two beers, he found that Lydia and the Cowboy were seated at a table next to them. The Cowboy was smiling and whispering into Lydia's ear, while she laughed in return.

'I don't like it,' Tuck muttered. 'It looks like she's enjoying herself too much!'

'She's just playing a role,' Jack murmured.

'What was that?' asked Wendy.

'A mantra,' Jack said hastily. 'I was saying a mantra to myself.'

'Wow,' said Wendy. 'I really didn't know you were into meditation, Jack. Seems like I don't really know much about you at all. I know I've been real mean in the past. I'm know I'm a real pain sometimes. It's probably on account of my life sucking the way it does. I'm a complete mess, you know . . . But I really *like* you, Jack. I mean, despite everything, I think I'm *attracted* to you.'

Jack listened to much more in this vein from her. In the past, the merest hint of a compliment would have delighted him. But now he was beginning to feel that he didn't have to prove anything to her.

Suddenly Wendy's ceaseless flow of words faltered. She was peering over his shoulder.

'That lady is signalling to you,' she said.

Jack looked around. Lydia was standing alone at the bar, gesturing to him. He rose and went over to her.

In a hushed and urgent voice she said, 'I found out something. He's meeting Scrimshaw early this morning —'

'This morning?' Jack said, puzzled.

'It's three A.M. already,' she told him. 'They're picking him up at the hotel. They're going to give him the chip they stole from Vectorscope.'

Jack was about to reply when the Cowboy appeared. He sidled up to Lydia.

'Cowboy,' she said, 'this is Jack, an old friend of mine.'

'Hi, Cowboy,' Jack said.

'Howdy, Big Jack,' the Cowboy said in a thick accent. He turned to Lydia: 'Let's go Buffalo Gal! Let's split this nowhere scene!'

Then he swept Lydia away through the crowd.

'*Let's split this nowhere scene*!' came Tuck's voice. 'That guy's slang is twenty years out of date!'

'What shall we do?' Jack asked.

'Follow them of course!' Tuck told him. 'Don't let them out of your sight!'

Jack hurried past Wendy's table towards the exit.

'Sorry,' he called to her. 'Gotta go.'

She gave a small rueful shrug.

Outside Jack clambered into the Mustang as Lydia and the Cowboy were driven away in a cab.

'Hurry up!' Tuck called to him.

He started the engine, revved it, and roared away.

102

Several minutes later the cab pulled up outside the hotel with Jack not far behind. Lydia and the Cowboy went inside.

'Come on,' Tuck said urgently as Jack found a parking space. 'Don't leave her alone in the hotel room with that guy!'

'Listen,' said Jack, 'I don't want them together any more than you do!'

'Yeah, okay,' said Tuck. 'Wait a minute – why not?'

'Because I don't trust him either, that's why!' Jack felt a surge of anger far stronger than any he had experienced before. If the Cowboy tried anything with Lydia, he'd . . . he wouldn't be responsible for his actions!

'Come on!' Tuck urged him again as he hurried towards the hotel entrance.

'Shut the heck up, will you!' Jack shouted angrily. 'I've had just about enough of your nagging for one day!' If Tuck had been standing in front of him at that moment, he was sure he would have hit him. The thought made him feel slightly ashamed. But only slightly.

'Why do I feel so hostile towards you all of a sudden?' he wondered aloud.

Tuck had an answer he wasn't expecting: 'I'm using the pod's computer to stimulate your adrenal gland, that's why. We gotta get that adrenalin pumping if you're going to play hero.'

Despite this, Jack wasn't convinced that Tuck's manipulations of his biochemistry were wholly the cause.

'Maybe that's the reason,' he said belligerently, 'and maybe it isn't.'

There was a pause, and then Tuck said, 'If you've got something to say, then say it.'

'She deserves better,' Jack blurted, 'that's all!'

'What d'you mean "better"? Better than *what*?'

'Better than *you*!'

Jack was now in the foyer, waiting for the elevator.

'I knew it!' Tuck said. 'You think she's got the hots for you, don't you?'

Jack said nothing. The elevator's doors opened and he stepped inside and pressed the floor button.

'You know what she sees in you?' Jack was saying. 'She sees *me*, that's who!'

Jack was boiling mad by now. 'That does it, Pendelton!' he shouted. 'Where are you?' He began to pound his body with his fist. 'I'm gonna throttle you!'

'Save it for the Cowboy!' Tuck said.

The doors opened and Jack surged out, rushing down the corridor to the Cowboy's door. Without pausing to knock, he raised his foot and kicked it open.

Inside the Cowboy was standing there in his shirt and socks, but no jeans. He was still wearing his hat. Before he could say or do anything, Jack punched him so hard on the jaw that he was knocked back on to the bed, unconscious.

'Attaboy!' Tuck shouted triumphantly. 'You did it, Jack. You did it!'

Suddenly Lydia rushed in from the corridor, still fully dressed.

'What happened?' she asked, surveying the Cowboy on the bed.

Jack was confused. 'Where were you?'

'Next door. In my room.'

'Ooops.'

'Beauty of a punch, anyway,' Tuck told him.

'Jack,' said Lydia, 'what's going on?'

Jack thought fast. 'Don't worry, it's all part of my plan.' Then, under his breath, he murmured to Tuck: 'We *do* have a plan, don't we?'

'You betcha!' said Tuck.

Under Tuck's directions, Jack hauled the Cowboy off the bed and dragged him into the bathroom. Then he proceeded to strip the Cowboy to his underwear before tying him up and gagging him with clothing taken from Tuck's case.

'What now?' Jack asked.

'Tell Lydia you want a few minutes alone. Then lock the bathroom door.'

Lydia was still in the bedroom. Jack did as he was ordered.

'Now you get changed,' Tuck said. 'You put on the Cowboy's clothes.'

'What?'

'You heard me. Put them on.'

'What for?'

'Just do as I say. Then afterwards I want you to stare hard at the Cowboy's face. I want to try something.'

Jack decided that it was futile to argue. Swiftly he stripped down to his underwear before putting on the Cowboy's shirt, blue jeans, leather boots and finally his hat. Then he peered at the Cowboy's face.

'What's all this about?' he finally asked Tuck.

'We planned an experiment,' Tuck told him. 'Something called the Nerve/Muscle/Gland Motor Response Adjustment. I'm going to try it out on you now.'

'You're what!' Jack said.

Inside the pod, Tuck was busy setting dials and flipping switches. As Jack focused on the Cowboy's face, Tuck froze the image on the monitor, then punched a few more buttons. The image turned into a computer analogue comprising straight lines and grid squares. Underneath the ghostly outline of the Cowboy's face remained. The grid proceeded to fold itself over the image until it conformed to the contours of the Cowboy's face.

'It boils down to an electronic stimulation of the nerves and muscles,' Tuck told Jack. 'If I can, I'm going to alter your appearance.'

He threw a lever.

Jack didn't like the sound of this one little bit. He panicked and ran for the door, forgetting that it was locked. He began to fumble with the bolt, but then he began to feel a twisting and a wrenching in his face.

He staggered back, and saw himself in the mirror above the washbasin.

The proportions of his face had begun to bulge, the forehead swelling, the bridge of his nose growing larger, the chin taking on a squarer appearance. His cheeks began to ripple in a perfectly horrific way.

'Oh my God!' Jack murmured. 'What are you doing to me?!'

His eyes began to pulse and throb. They turned a deeper shade of brown. A prickling started up all over his scalp, and suddenly his hair had gone darker and rearranged itself under the Cowboy's hat. It was unbelievable. Jack began to scream.

'Jack!' Lydia shouted through the door. 'What's happening? Are you all right?'

There was a cracking, stretching sound, and Jack's

nose became flatter. His lips curled, grew fatter. Even his complexion altered.

The real Cowboy awoke in the bath. When he saw what was happening, he fainted dead away.

'Help me!' Jack began to shout as the cracking continued and his cheekbones became distinctly more sculptured.

'We're almost done, Jack,' said Tuck. Just a few adjustments to the forehead and eyebrows . . .'

Two waves of pain surged out from Jack's temples, and he howled. His eyebrows rippled as if they were infested with lice. He staggered back, closing his eyes.

Then everything went quiet. All the pain, the movement stopped. Cautiously Jack opened his eyes – and gasped when he saw the Cowboy peering back at him from the mirror.

'You . . . you *brute*!' Jack said to Tuck. 'What have you done to me? You've turned me into the Cowboy! I'll never forgive you!'

'Easy, Jack. It's only a temporary effect, I promise. It's part of my plan.'

'Your plan!' Jack shouted. 'You've turned me into a *mutant*!'

'No, Jack. Just calm down a minute, will you? Calm down and listen . . .'

Soon afterwards the bathroom door opened. Lydia gasped when the Cowboy walked out. She began to back away.

'It's me, Lydia,' Jack said. It was a small relief to him that his voice had scarcely been altered by the 'experiment'.

And Lydia recognized it. 'Jack?' she said.

'It's me,' he told her again. 'I'm Jack. I've just got the Cowboy's face.'

She kept backing away. 'But how . . .?'

'Don't ask, Lydia. Just keep trusting me. I'll explain everything later, I promise, but not right now.'

She continued to peer at him suspiciously.

'You do believe it's me, don't you?' he asked.

She still looked uncertain.

'Take a look in the bathroom,' he told her. 'The *real* Cowboy's still trussed up in there. I changed into his clothes.'

Very cautiously, Lydia went past him and peered inside. The Cowboy was still out cold.

'I don't understand,' Lydia said, thoroughly shaken. 'I don't understand any of this.'

'It's part of the plan,' Jack told her. 'Scrimshaw is due soon. We're going to fool him into thinking that I'm the Cowboy.'

10

'They'll be here soon,' Jack said to Lydia.

'I know,' she replied.

'It's going to be dangerous.'

'I know.'

'You don't have to stay. I can handle it.'

Jack wasn't sure he meant this, and in any case Lydia shook her head adamantly.

'I'm coming with you,' she insisted.

'There's no need – ' Jack began, but then Tuck's irritated voice broke in: 'What is this? Your noble half-hour?'

'I'm just trying to protect her,' Jack murmured under his breath.

'What?' said Lydia.

Jack shook his head at her. 'I've got this habit of mumbling to myself.'

'If you ask me,' she said, 'there's a lot of things that are more than a little strange about you.'

'She can take care of herself,' Tuck said. 'You're gonna need all the help you can get.'

There was a knock on the door.

Jack and Lydia exchanged glances before Jack rose and opened it. Two men were standing outside.

'Mr Scrimshaw is waiting,' one of them said.

'Good,' Jack replied. He indicated Lydia. 'She's coming along, too. Let's hit the trail.'

He had been practising his accent, and did a reasonably good imitation of the Cowboy's speech. Neither of the henchmen seemed to object to Lydia accompanying him. As they went out, Jack slipped the DO NOT DISTURB sign on the door.

They were driven to Scrimshaw's in a black Volvo sedan. Scrimshaw's Rolls Royce was parked outside. A pale grey dawn had broken over the city by now, and inside the pod, Tuck checked his watch: six o'clock. Only three hours of air left.

The henchmen led them into a long glassed-in veranda where palms abounded. A large table had been set for breakfast, and around it sat Scrimshaw, Margaret Canker, and several henchmen. Nearby, a friendly-looking Golden Retriever was curled restfully on the floor near its food dish.

Scrimshaw rose on seeing them. He was dressed in an elegant cream summer suit.

'Good morning, Cowboy,' he said, smiling. 'Come in. Sit down. Join us.'

His manner was so friendly that Jack muttered under his breath: 'Do you think we're close friends?'

'God,' said Tuck, 'I hope not.'

'And who is this?' Scrimshaw asked pleasantly as Jack led Lydia up to the table.

'Lydia Maxwell,' Jack told him. 'A friend of mine.'

Scrimshaw took Lydia's hands and kissed it in a rather smarmy manner. He gave Jack a 'we're-all-men-of-the-world' look, as if to suggest that no further explanation of her presence was necessary.

'How long has it been, Cowboy?' Scrimshaw asked as seats were provided for them.

'Uh . . .' said Jack, fighting down a tremor of panic. 'You tell me.'

'Almost six years.' Scrimshaw took a mouthful of coffee and savoured it before saying, 'Don't you remember? It was at Idi Amin's barbeque.'

Jack forced a smile. 'Oh, yes. How could I forget?'

Someone's foot stroked his leg under the table. It was Margaret Canker's.

'You haven't forgotten the last time *we* saw each other, have you, Cowboy?'

Jack gave another uncomfortable smile. Canker winked at him. He winked back.

'You look different, Cowboy,' Scrimshaw observed. 'Do I?'

'Thinner. You've lost weight.'

'I've been sick,' Jack improvised.

'Good one!' Tuck said from within.

'I'm sorry to hear that,' Scrimshaw said.

'Yeah,' Jack went on, unable to resist it, 'I just haven't been myself lately.'

'Okay,' Tuck said. 'Quit while you're ahead!'

Scrimshaw signalled to a waiter, and he approached with a coffee pot. Jack and Lydia both nodded for their empty cups to be filled. Jack gazed around the table at the decidedly unfriendly faces of Scrimshaw's henchmen. Everybody seemed to be watching him. To begin with, he had almost enjoyed the masquerade, but now he wasn't so sure he could carry it off.

Scrimshaw produced two cigars from his pocket.

'Do join me,' he said, offering Jack one. 'I believe these are the kind you like . . . Cuban?'

Jack didn't know a panatella from a pancake. He'd tried to smoke a cigar as a kid, and it had made him feel nauseous.

111

'You're in luck,' Tuck said. 'Cuban cigars are the *best*.'

Jack slipped the cigar into his pocket, saying, 'I think I'll save it for later.'

Scrimshaw made a gesture as if to say that it was all the same to him.

'Very well then,' he said, 'so much for the pleasantries. Let's get down to business.' He turned to Canker and said, 'Would you fill the Cowboy in, Dr Canker, on the details of the process.'

She cleared her throat. 'Miniaturization works on a dual-chip system. We have one chip in our possession at the moment. We will have the other one shortly.'

Both she and Scrimshaw regarded Jack with a slight measure of concern, as though anticipating that only one chip would not be good enough for the Cowboy.

'Take what they've got,' Tuck advised Jack.

'Fine,' Jack said aloud. 'I'll take what you've got.'

Scrimshaw and Canker exchanged a glance.

'You *do* understand,' Canker said, 'that the first chip only miniaturizes. *Both* chips are required for re-enlargement.'

'I understand,' Jack replied. 'It will have to do for now. I'll whet my customer's appetite with what we've got.'

'Good point,' said Tuck from within.

'Good point,' Scrimshaw said, smiling. He turned back to Canker. 'Show him the chip.'

Canker produced a small gold pillbox from the pocket of her lab coat. She opened it and held up the chip with a pair of surgical tweezers.

Inside the pod, Tuck stared at the chip on his display monitor. There it was, his only hope of salvation. He

112

felt an intense frustration that he could not simply reach out and grab it. But he controlled himself, and said to Jack: 'Easy, now. *That's* what we need.'

Jack and Lydia were both trying to hide their excitement from Scrimshaw and his cronies. As casually as possible, Jack reached out to take the chip. But Scrimshaw put a hand on his arm.

'I wonder,' he said to Lydia, 'if the Cowboy has ever told you of his incredible tolerance for pain.'

Lydia frowned. 'His *what*?'

Scrimshaw smiled. 'It's quite remarkable, isn't it, Cowboy? Your stoicism is legendary, and I'm surprised you haven't apprised your companion of the fact. Hiding your light under a bushel, eh? That's so unlike you, Cowboy.' The smile broadened, became more menacing. 'If that *is* who you are!'

Grabbing Jack's wrist, Scrimshaw slammed it down on the table. Jack was more startled than hurt, but now everyone at the table apart from Lydia was glaring at him suspiciously.

Scrimshaw motioned to a henchman, who approached. Scrimshaw whispered into his ear, and the henchman went inside the house. Still Jack's hand was flattened against the table, Scrimshaw holding it down. The pot of coffee had overturned, and the hot black liquid began to run towards Jack's hand. Both he and Scrimshaw watched it. By the time it touched Jack's wrist, it had cooled to a bearable temperature, and Jack did not even flinch.

Scrimshaw was obviously impressed, and Jack thought that he had passed the test. But then there was a flaring noise behind him as Scrimshaw said, 'You don't mind if I satisfy my curiosity for myself, do you?'

Igoe had appeared from the house. At the end of his false arm was an acetylene torch, a pale blue flame jetting out from its end.

'No!' Lydia shouted as Igoe stepped toward Jack. 'Don't!'

She tried to rise from her chair, but a henchman pushed her back. Jack began to struggle frantically to free his hand from Scrimshaw's grip.

'Don't worry,' Scrimshaw told him, 'Dr Canker here is a pioneer in the field of limb replacement.'

Igoe brought the flame to within a few inches of Jack's head. Jack surged to his feet, but two henchmen grabbed him and forced him down again. He began to grapple with them, pure terror filling his whole being.

'Jack!' Tuck called from within. 'You're generating too much electrical energy. I can't hold the balance!'

Jack didn't hear him. He was struggling with all his might, wrenching and twisting his body in an effort to get free as Igoe brought the torch close once more. Then suddenly he felt his face beginning to bulge and warp. Igoe stepped back in surprise, and Scrimshaw's determined expression changed rapidly into one of alarm. He staggered back from his chair, saying, 'Cowboy, no more! It was only a joke! Only a joke!'

The henchman fell away as Jack's face pulsed and rippled with increasing rapidity. Everyone started to scream.

'Cowboy!' yelled Scrimshaw. 'I beg of you! Please stop!'

Jack could do nothing except moan with pain as his whole face began to vibrate and buckle and swell. Inside him, Tuck was frantically trying to dampen down the effect, but it was out of control. His features kept

114

distorting with terrifying rapidity, and even Lydia was shocked. Cups overturned on the table, muffins and toast and pots of marmalade were scattered to the floor as everyone began retreating.

Then, with a terrific snap, Jack's face collapsed back to normal.

There were more screams. But they swiftly abated when everyone saw that the bizarre changes had finally ceased.

'It's him!' Scrimshaw shouted. 'It's Jack Putter.' Rapidly regaining his aplomb, he turned to his henchmen: 'Get him!'

The chip had fallen on the table. Jack, only dimly aware of what had happened, snatched it up as the henchmen started towards him. Lydia, the only person who had stood her ground beside Jack, reacted swiftly, up-ending the table in their faces. More crockery and cutlery went flying, along with the remains of the breakfast. The henchmen began to slip on the solarium's tiled floor.

'He's got the chip!' Scrimshaw was screaming. 'Stop him! Stop him!'

Igoe leapt in front of Jack, blocking his path.

'Lydia,' Jack shouted. 'Catch!'

He tossed the chip towards her, but it fell short, dropping into the golden retriever's dish with a soft plop. Igoe threw his arms around Jack, locking him in a bear-hug.

Scrimshaw pushed the inquisitive dog away from its dish before going down on his hands and knees and rooting through the mushy dog-food with his bare hands. Finally he located the chip and held it up triumphantly. It was covered with sticky red-brown dog-food.

'Don't kill him!' Scrimshaw ordered Igoe. 'Lock him up. The girl, too.'

Two henchmen had already grabbed Lydia. Igoe released Jack, and he slithered limply to the floor.

Jack and Lydia were taken and locked away in a cellar room. Barred sunlight shone in through the gaps in the slatted roof overhead. Jack urgently began looking around for some means of escape. Lydia watched him but didn't move.

'We've got to get out of here!' Jack said to her. 'Don't just stand there! Help!'

She shook her head. 'Not until you tell me what's going on! I want to know *everything*, Jack. Right now!'

Jack ceased his pacing and regarded her.

'Tell her,' Tuck said from within. 'We've got nothing to lose now.'

To Lydia, Jack said, 'You won't believe me.'

'Try me,' she insisted. 'You're forgetting that I've seen your face change totally twice in the last few hours. I'll believe anything after that!'

11

'I don't believe it,' Lydia said when Jack had finished telling her everything.

'I told you you wouldn't,' Jack replied.

'Tell her I'm disappointed in her,' Tuck said from within.

'No,' Jack said to him. 'Did you really expect she would?'

'Wait a minute,' said Lydia. 'You're talking to him now, aren't you? And before – that's what you were doing, not mumbling to yourself, isn't it? The whole thing's so incredible it has to be true.' She looked confused, then shook her head. 'No, it can't be – it's *too* crazy.'

'That's female logic for you,' Tuck said.

Jack repeated this to Lydia. Again she began to look half-convinced, remarking, 'That's just the sort of thing Tuck would say.'

'Jack,' Tuck said from inside, 'repeat to Lydia my exact words, will you?'

'Okay,' said Jack.

He listened to Tuck while Lydia waited expectantly. Then he repeated the message: 'Lydia, I don't blame you for leaving me that morning. But it *was* my heart that was broken and not my toe.' Jack looked confused. 'What the heck is that supposed to mean?'

Jack did not understand the message, but he immediately saw that Lydia was finally convinced. Her mouth dropped open and her eyes moistened.

Gazing at Jack, she whispered, 'Tuck . . . Tuck . . . it really *is* you, isn't it?'

Then she threw her arms around Jack's neck.

Jack reacted with alarm. Unsure of what to do with Lydia's arms, he prised them free and stepped back.

'Okay!' he said. 'Wait a minute here!'

Lydia looked perplexed, but Jack had actually *enjoyed* having her arms around his neck. He wanted to savour it without feeling that someone else was watching. 'Tuck,' he said, 'I want a moment alone.'

'Huh?' said Tuck. He was presently guiding the pod up Jack's throat towards his mouth.

'Shut down your sensors,' Jack said. 'No sound. No picture.'

Tuck immediately understood why he wanted this.

'Bad idea, Jack,' he said. 'I'd be navigating in the dark. What if I couldn't restore contact afterwards? No, Jack, I can't do that.'

'I want a moment alone,' Jack insisted with uncharacteristic firmness.

'Alone with *Lydia,* you mean!'

'You owe me this, Tuck!'

Tuck thought about it, studying Lydia on the screen. She looked adorable, but she said nothing.

'Okay,' Tuck said abruptly. 'Signing off.' And he shut down.

Jack could feel a slight change in his body, he was sure. It was a sudden sensation of freedom, of being his own man again. He grinned, then stepped forward and took Lydia's hands in his own.

'Lydia,' he said, 'I'm not sure what I have to say to you. I've only known you for less than a day, but – '

He stopped short as the sound of footsteps coming down the cellar stairs could be heard.

Swiftly Jack seized the moment, knowing that he might never get another chance. Before Lydia could protest, he drew her forward and planted a big kiss on her lips. It was an urgent, passionate kiss, and her mouth opened wide in response. To Jack, it was simply delicious.

Then the door was thrown open. Jack broke the kiss and stepped back. One of the henchmen was framed in the doorway.

'Let's go!' he shouted.

Inside the pod, Tuck was frantically attempting to restore communication with Jack, but both sound and vision remained dead.

'Jack?' Tuck said. 'Do you read me? Damn! I knew I shouldn't have shut down my sensors!'

Under heavy guard, Jack and Lydia were driven swiftly through San Francisco until they came to Margaret Canker's laboratory complex. Canker, Igoe and Scrimshaw had followed in another car, and Canker immediately ordered that Lydia be taken to her office. Then Jack was led through to her lab.

Technicians were standing at the ready while Jack was taken to a stainless steel table and lashed down. A plastic collar which resembled a neck brace was snapped around his neck. At its front was a small metal nozzle with a hole in its centre.

'What's going on!' Jack shouted. 'Let me go!'

He had been struggling ever since he had been taken

from the car, but the henchmen had kept him firmly in their grasp. And now he was unable to move, the straps on the table holding him fast.

'Prepare the miniaturizer,' Canker said calmly to the technicians. Turning to Scrimshaw, she went on: 'We'll use the chip we already have to miniaturize Igoe, then inject him into Putter. He'll locate the pod, eliminate its pilot by whatever means necessary, take command of it and retrieve the second chip.'

Jack began to struggle more frantically, but it was hopeless.

'Tuck?' he murmured under his breath. 'Tuck? Where are you?'

There was no response.

Tuck was unaware that Jack was calling him. He was taking the pod down a dark glistening tunnel lit only by the pod's searchlights.

'Where am I?' he wondered aloud, punching the audio and visual links yet again. Still they gave him no sound or vision. Then the computer voice spoke: 'You are presently located in the oesophagus.'

'Right,' Tuck said immediately. There was only one thing for it. 'Give me a route to the optic nerve again. I'm going to have to plant another remote.'

Meanwhile, in the laboratory, Margaret Canker pulled a hose down from a piece of equipment above Jack. Attached to the end of the hose was a hypodermic syringe. Ignoring Jack's protests, she inserted the needle of the syringe into the hole of the metal nozzle in Jack's collar.

Jack heard a noise off to his right. He managed to twist his head around a little and saw Igoe inside a futuristic-looking diving suit. He was being loaded by pulley into a black one-man craft with two arms that terminated in large mechanical pincers.

Once inside, a hatch was clamped down over him. Jack saw him peering out through the viewscreen. He clicked the pincers tauntingly.

'Engage PEM,' Canker said.

Meanwhile, Tuck had managed to deploy the optic remote. The monitor screen lit up, showing the face of a henchman and a surrounding office. The scene didn't alter for several minutes. Frustrated, Tuck followed his previous route to the ear-drum, where he deployed another remote.

On the screen he suddenly saw a hand – a *woman's* hand – reach for a purse which he recognized as Lydia's. The henchman snatched it away just as the audio link came on line:

'I was just getting some gum.'

It was Lydia's voice. He was inside *her*!

Tuck was too startled to think. He saw the henchman smile shrewdly, then say, 'After I check the purse for nail files.'

He pushed his hand into the purse, and there was a sudden ZIPP-BUZZ. His face screwed up in pain, and he withdrew his hand to reveal a stun dart sticking into his palm.

'A shame,' Lydia said calmly. 'That was my last dart, too.'

The henchman's eyes closed, and he went rigid.

Lydia didn't waste time. Picking up the phone on the desk, she dialled Duane Flornoy's number. The phone rang and rang, then finally Duane answered.

'Duane!' Lydia said with relief. 'Thank God it's you!'

'What's up, Lydia? You sound fraught.'

'I don't have time to explain now. But you've got to reach Vectorscope. This is *very* important. Tell them I've got Tuck Pendelton and I'm attempting to bring him in.' She told him where the lab was located. 'Call the police out.'

'Got it,' said Flornoy, obviously bewildered. 'Lydia, are you in as much trouble as you sound?'

'Maybe more,' she told him, then hung up.

She glanced around the office, saw Canker's lab coat hanging on a hook and put it on. Then she took the pistol from the paralysed henchman before hurrying out.

There was no one in the corridor. She crept down to the door of the main lab.

'Attaboy, Lydia,' Tuck said.

She froze, whispered, 'Tuck?'

'It's me. I'm in you now.'

'But how . . .?'

'Somehow I got transferred from Jack. I guess it must have been when the two of you kissed.'

'Tuck, I can't believe it – '

'Listen, there's no time to wonder over it now. Just be careful, that's all! Time is short, so get in there!'

His urgency spurred Lydia over her astonishment. Cautiously opening the door, she crept inside unnoticed and stood there just like any other technician.

Jack, meanwhile, was feeling distinctly panic-striken. Igoe and his craft had been lowered into a chamber in the floor and a screen then drawn down over the hole. There had been a flash of light, and when the screen was withdrawn, the black craft had vanished. It had been miniaturized, and afterwards Canker had drawn

122

it into a hypodermic. Now she was going to inject it into him.

'Wait a minute,' Scrimshaw said. 'After Igoe takes command of the pod, how do we get the chip out?'

'He'll pilot the pod out through a tear-duct or sweat-gland,' Canker told him.

'Why chance it?' Scrimshaw said. 'As soon as he takes over the pod and gets the chip, *let's re-enlarge!*'

Canker peered at him. 'While it's still *inside* Mr Putter?'

'Sure.'

Another jolt of terror surged through Jack at the thought.

'Do you have any idea,' Canker was saying, 'what kind of mess that would make?'

'Hey!' Jack screamed. 'Hey! You can't do this to me!'

Both Canker and Scrimshaw ignored him.

'Tuck!' he cried, struggling against his bindings. 'Tuck! Give me more adrenalin! Make me strong, Tuck!'

He began to strain hard against his bonds, using all the strength in his body, feeling more powerful than he had ever done before.

SNAP! SNAP! SNAP!

Jack surged upright. He yanked the hose from the collar.

'He's loose!' Scrimshaw yelled. 'Grab him!'

Several technicians darted forward and seized Jack. He struggled manfully, but there were too many of them.

Pinned down again, Jack could do nothing to prevent Canker from inserting the needle into his collar. Lydia was fumbling for her gun, but too late. Canker pressed the plunger of the hypodermic, and Jack felt fluid gush into one of the veins in his neck.

'He's in!' Canker said triumphantly. 'Igoe's in!'

Lydia pulled out the pistol and fired it into the air.

'Let go of him!' she yelled.

Everyone in the lab jumped. Lydia levelled the pistol. The technicians immediately backed away. Wrenching off the collar, Jack jumped down and hurried over to her.

'What do we do now?' Lydia whispered to him. 'I haven't got enough bullets for all of them.'

'Don't worry,' Jack whispered back. Then he shouted to the others: 'Everybody into the miniaturizer!'

For a moment no one moved. Canker managed to reach out and twist a dial on the control panel.

'Don't touch that!' Lydia shouted. She fired the pistol over Canker's head. Canker, Scrimshaw and the technicians hastily scrambled down into the chamber in the laboratory floor.

Lydia and Jack darted over to the control panel. Jack pressed a switch, and the screen began to descend over the hole.

'This is all your fault, Margaret,' Scrimshaw was fuming.

'Shut up,' she told him. 'I managed to bring the dial up to fifty per cent.'

'What does *that* mean?'

'It means we won't be shrunk to the size of a virus. We'll only be – '

Her further words were cut off as the screen closed

over them. The miniaturizer started automatically: there was a hum and a whine, then a flash of light.

'Let's go!' said Lydia.

'Wait!' said Jack. 'The chip!'

He tried to pluck it free from the control board, but without success. In frustration he shouted, 'Gimme the damned chip!' and slammed his hand against the panel.

With this, the voice-activated robotic arm descended and delicately removed the chip before offering it to Jack with all the finesse of a highly trained waiter.

Jack and Lydia hurried out, slamming a heavy metal door behind them.

The patrol car came screeching to a halt, and two officers jumped out, their guns at the ready. They were responding to Duane Flornoy's call, and they entered the laboratory building cautiously, moving slowly down the corridor towards the main lab.

Pushing open the swinging doors, they entered, holding their pistols before them in a two-handed grip. The place looked deserted. Then they heard sounds coming from a chamber set into the floor. Voices.

'Press the yellow button!' came a woman's voice above the others. 'The yellow button!'

Very carefully, the officers moved across to the patrol panel. One of them saw the yellow button. Not knowing what else to do, he pressed it.

The screen drew back from the floor. The two policemen gaped and backed away with sheer incredulity as several figures clambered out. Two of them – a white-haired man and a woman – immediately scurried out of the lab. The policemen were too stunned to move.

'Are you seeing what I'm seeing?' one said to the other, staring down at the white-coated figures who remained.

'Yeah,' the other replied. 'But I don't believe it.'

12

Jack and Lydia emerged in an alleyway at the rear of the lab. Suddenly a henchman appeared in front of them, blocking the way.

Lydia backed off, but Jack was undaunted.

'Don't worry,' he told her. 'Tuck's giving me the strength of ten men.'

And he surged forward before Lydia was able to explain that Tuck was now inside her.

The fight was brief. Jack waded in, fists flying, and the henchman was quickly overwhelmed by the sheer confidence and energy of his attack. Under a battery of punches, he fell dazed to the alley floor.

It was the same man who had driven them to the lab in the black Volvo. Jack searched through his pockets and found a set of car keys.

The Volvo man parked beside an outbuilding nearby. Its doors were already unlocked.

'Listen,' Lydia said as they climbed in, 'before you drive off, there's something you ought to know.'

Jack started the car. 'What?'

'Tuck's inside me now.'

'*What?*'

'He was transferred across when we kissed. He's been talking to me, and he can see through my eyes.'

Jack immediately knew that she was telling the truth. Tuck hadn't been in contact with him since they were locked in Scrimshaw's cellar. Since the kiss . . .

'That means . . .' he began. 'The guy in the alley . . .'

'That's right,' Lydia said, grinning. 'You took him out all by yourself!'

Immediately Jack's fist began to throb with pain from a punch he'd landed to the henchman's jaw. He couldn't credit how stupid he'd been. Yet at the same time, there was no denying he *had* pummelled the guy into submission without anyone's help.

The car started with a roar, and Jack drove off like a fury.

Lydia was silent for a while. Then she said, 'I want you to kiss me again.'

'Huh?' said Jack.

'Tuck says its the only way. Igoe is inside you, and Jack has to stop him.'

Before Jack could argue, Lydia reached forward and thrust her lips over his. Jack did his best to keep steering the Volvo in a straight line as their lips parted. It was incredible to think that at that instant – hopefully – Tuck and the pod were being transferred from one body to another.

Inside the pod, Tuck was swept through from Lydia to Jack down into the chasm of Jack's throat.

'Here I am again!' he shouted into the radio.

'Tuck's back!' Jack said aloud for Lydia's benefit.

'Step on the gas,' Lydia said, checking her watch. 'It's almost eight-thirty!'

Unseen by Jack and Lydia, the Volvo passed a Dodge Dart going in the opposite direction. It was being driven by Pete Blanchard, and he spotted them. Immediately he made a fast U-turn.

* * *

Tuck heard the BEEP of a sonar blip on his display monitor. He regarded it, wondering what he was going to do. Presumably Igoe also had sonar aboard his pod so that he would also know where Tuck was.

Tuck was parked on the 'ledge' between the two openings that led to the stomach and lungs. He sat very still, his eyes shifting in all directions as the bleep of the sonar grew louder. Igoe was closing fast.

Minutes passed in silence. Tuck was tempted to talk to Jack to ask for further details of Igoe's craft, but he couldn't allow anything to break his concentration now.

Then, without warning, Igoe suddenly rose up from the depths of the oesophagus.

His craft was like a huge mechanical lobster with two grasping arms. Through its viewer Igoe was smiling at Tuck from within his suit.

The pincers swiftly clamped down on the pod and began to rock it violently. Tuck, strapped into his seat, was thrown around like a man on a bucking bronco. He managed to manipulate the pod's arms so that it gripped the 'ledge', stabilizing it.

The stability didn't last long. Igoe used a pincer to snip off one of the arms. The pod lurched and slipped to the brink of the ledge. Below was the dark, pulsating tunnel which led down to the stomach.

Meanwhile, Jack was driving as fast as possible towards the Vectorscope laboratories. They had only twenty-five minutes in which to save Tuck. Suddenly a voice called from behind: 'Stop the car!'

Scrimshaw and Canker rose up from the back seat. They were only half their normal size.

Jack and Lydia both gasped. Jack recalled Canker fiddling with the dial of the miniaturizer before they had been shrunk. Somehow Canker and Scrimshaw had escaped from the chamber after being reduced to half-size. They must have climbed into the Volvo and hidden in the back seat while he was beating up the guy in the alleyway.

'Stop the car!' Scrimshaw shouted again.

'Floor it!' yelled Lydia.

Jack put his foot on the gas and the car surged forward. Canker and Scrimshaw were flung back on top of each other.

Lydia twisted around in her seat just as Scrimshaw flung himself toward Jack and tried to pluck the key from the ignition. Canker grabbed Lydia around the neck, and Lydia was forced into the back seat to wrestle with her. The Volvo began to weave all over the road as Jack struggled with Scrimshaw.

Scrimshaw stood up in Jack's lap, blocking his view of the road. He clamped his hands around Jack's throat and tried to throttle him.

Inside Jack, this choking motion caused Jack's oesophagus to bulge inwards, knocking Igoe's craft from the ledge. It fell down the dark pit towards the stomach.

Jack pushed Scrimshaw off his lap and veered to avoid a car directly in his path. The Volvo skidded along a beach-side road, then bounced down a set of steps. Inside Jack, Tuck was also bouncing furiously.

The car came to a halt on the beach. Lydia flung Canker against the seat and clambered out, following Jack. Blanchard's Dodge roared up and parked at the top of the steps.

'Lydia!' he called out.

She looked up. Blanchard was wearing sunglasses, and it was a second before she recognized him.

'C'mon,' he called. 'Get in the car!'

She and Jack ran to it and jumped in the back seat.

Inside Jack, Igoe's craft was whirling out of control as it plummeted down the oesophagus. The steering had been damaged and wouldn't respond. Igoe slipped out of his seat harness, pulled down his face mask, then pressed a button marked EJECT.

The hatch bolts exploded and Igoe was blasted back up the oesophagus at tremendous speed as the damaged craft continued falling towards the stomach.

Within the pod, Tuck was startled to see Igoe's sonar blip race back on to the screen. Igoe surged into view, hitting the pod with a THUD and holding on.

Through the viewscreen, Tuck saw Igoe peering inside with an expression of pure madness. He pulled off a glove to reveal an industrial drill attachment. It began to whirr loudly. He worked his way towards the pod's air tanks.

Tuck immediately pulled back on the pod's control stick. It banked sharply to the left, then to the right. Tuck was trying to shake Igoe off, but he clung tenaciously on, drilling at the tanks.

Then Tuck had an idea.

'Jack!' he said. 'Are you nervous?'

Jack was sitting in the back of Pete Blanchard's car, having his fevered brow stroked by Lydia as Blanchard drove speedily in the direction of Vectorscope.

'Actually,' Jack said, breathing in deeply, 'I'm feeling pretty calm at the moment, thank you.'

'No good, Jack! I need stomach acid. Lots of it!'

131

Jack shook his head. 'No! Leave me alone! I've had enough anxiety for one day!'

'Jack, it's urgent!'

'No!' Jack insisted. 'Leave me alone!'

Tuck was about to shout again, but then he thought of a better tactic.

'Jack,' he said softly, 'I don't want to alarm you, but I saw something funny in here.'

He allowed a pause. Jack said, 'What do you mean – something funny?'

'Well, it's probably benign. A biopsy will tell.'

'What do you mean? Is it a tumour? My God, how big is it?'

'You're asking the wrong guy, Jack. To me, it's the size of a mountain – '

'Oh my God!'

Jack clutched his stomach in panic. Tuck, grinning evilly, immediately put the pod into motion.

'Attaboy, Jack,' he called. 'Keep those stomach acids flowing!' And then, addressing Igoe, he said, 'Hang on, buddy – here's how I spell *acid relief*!'

The pod plunged down the dark tunnel of the œsophagus towards the now-seething pit of the stomach. Igoe, still clinging on, suddenly began to look alarmed.

The pod's searchlights revealed the bubbling acidic pool just a second before Tuck splashed straight into it, submerging.

The shell of the pod was of a non-metallic material, as Tuck knew well. It would be quite safe from Jack's gastric juices. Which was more than could be said for Igoe . . .

Through the viewscreen, Tuck could see Jack's stomach acid boiling around the pod. It was like being in a submarine, caught in a raging sea-storm. The pod bucked and rolled, but Tuck was safely strapped into his seat. Jack's digestive juices were cloudy, so that Tuck could see nothing of Igoe.

Presently the storm began to subside. Tuck took the pod up out of Jack's stomach. As it surfaced, he saw Igoe still hanging there – or what was left of him. Igoe's hand-drill was still sticking into the pod's surface, but of Igoe himself, nothing remained apart from a skeleton.

'Hey, Jack,' Tuck called, 'you just digested the bad guy!'

There was a dull explosion of sound as Jack burped.

Inside the telephone booth, Scrimshaw was sitting on Canker's shoulders. He had just managed to reach up and take the receiver off the hook.

'Dial 911,' Canker told him.

'The police?' said Scrimshaw. 'Are you crazy? I'm calling my lawyer.'

He took some coins from his pocket and slotted them in. But nothing happened.

'Dammit!' he cried. 'My pocket change is all shrunk! When is this going to wear off, Margaret?'

Canker said nothing, but her expression told him 'Never'.

'I'm damned if I'm going to be three foot high for the rest of my life!' he said defiantly.

'Look on the bright side, Victor,' Canker said. 'You're no longer a size 44 Extra Fat. Now you can go straight to size 32 children's.'

Scrimshaw growled like an angry animal. His claw-like hands moved down towards Canker's neck, but he restrained himself at the last moment.

Pete Blanchard's car roared into the parking lot at Vectorscope and came screeching to a halt.

'We made it,' Blanchard said, propping up his sun-glasses on his forehead. 'With *one full minute to spare.*'

Jack, Lydia and Blanchard hurried inside to the main lab. Dr Niles and his team of technicians were waiting for them.

'Fire up the boilers, doc!' Niles said.

Inside Jack, Tuck had taken the pod into one of Jack's lungs. The journey had been a slow one, for the pod had been damaged by Igoe's attack and would no longer move under full power.

'Jack,' Tuck said into the radio, 'you gotta sneeze for me. Can you do it, pal?'

'Eh?' said Jack. 'Sneeze? Why?'

'Because I don't have enough air left. The pod's on reduced power, and I can't reach your mouth or eyes in time. The human sneeze has been clocked at over one hundred miles per hour. I'm in your lung and my only chance to make it out is for you to sneeze!'

'Are you serious?'

'*Deadly* serious.'

'Okay . . . but *how*?'

'Think *allergies*!' Tuck said instantly. 'Think pollen! Think cat fur! Horse hair! Think fuzzy, itchy, scratchy things floating up your nose and down your throat.'

Jack thought about them, but nothing happened. There wasn't even the merest tickling in his nostrils.

'Think house dust!' Tuck said desperately. 'Think of

134

tiny mites scurrying through your nasal cavities! Think
. . . uh . . . uh . . .'

'Hair spray!' Jack shouted.

He began peering frantically around the lab.

'Somebody!' he yelled to the technicians. 'Anybody!
Please! I need hair spray! Now! HURRY!'

One of the women technicians produced a can from
her purse. Jack took it from her and blasted himself in
the face with the aerosol.

Immediately a furious itching began in his nose,
while his eyes filled with water.

'Ah . . . ahhh . . .' He began.

Inside the pod, Tuck braced himself. He could feel
the sneeze coming. The pod began to tremble as Jack's
respiratory system started to convulse.

'Ahhhhhh – CHOOOOOO!!'

Tuck was flattened in his seat as the pod rocketed up
Jack's trachea at a speed which turned everything
outside into a blur. He felt his face being contorted
under the stress of the thrust.

Outside, Pete Blanchard was peering closely at Jack
through his sunglasses. Suddenly Jack's sneeze splattered the lenses.

Blanchard stepped back in surprise. Niles snatched
the sunglasses off his face, and one of the technicians
pulled a magnifying glass from his white coat and
peered at the lenses.

'I see it!' he cried. 'I see the pod!'

'Quickly!' Niles said. 'We need the chip!'

Jack remembered that he had it. He dug deep in his
trouser pocket and pulled out his hand scattering the
contents of one of the lab benches.

Bits of lint and dust. Pennies. A ticket stub. An

aspirin tablet. The torn off strip of a cash receipt from the supermarket. Jack prodded it with his finger. Underneath it was the chip.

Quickly one of the technicians took it and fitted it into the control board with a pair of tweezers. The pod had already been placed inside the chamber and the protective screen had been closed.

Niles hesitated, as if unsure of what button to press.

'Come on!' Jack and Lydia shouted in unison.

Niles prodded one of the buttons.

Lights began to flash in the lab. There was a powerful high-pitched whistle which grew rapidly in intensity so that everyone was forced to cover their ears with their hands.

There was a flash of light, and then silence descended. Soon afterwards, the two halves of the protective screen drew back.

The pod sat on the platform, full-sized once more.

Igoe's skeleton still clung to it, but at that moment it slipped off and clattered to the floor. The pod dripped with gooey biochemical secretions.

Suddenly the hatch door burst open and Tuck poked his head out, gasping for air.

Everybody cheered.

Pete Blanchard was the first to greet Tuck as he stepped out of the pod, grubby and sweat-stained.

'Told you we'd get you out of there, Tuck!' Blanchard said.

Tuck merely gave him an ironic smile and walked past him to catch Lydia as she raced forward into his arms.

'Tuck!' Lydia cried. 'I was beginning to think I'd never see you alive again!'

'Without your help,' he said, 'I would never have made it.'

He hugged her hard, then, peering over her shoulder, saw Jack standing there. Gently he set Lydia back on her feet.

Jack came forward, producing Scrimshaw's Cuban cigar and offering it to him.

'Welcome home, Lieutenant.'

Tuck smiled, put the cigar into his pocket, then gave Jack a big bear hug. Everyone cheered again, and Lydia's eyes filled up with emotion.

Soon, everyone was clustered around Tuck, slapping him on the back and giving him their congratulations. But presently Tuck struggled free of the crowd and took Lydia aside.

'We have to talk in private,' he told her.

She nodded, and he took her into the observation room next door.

'I never got into space, Lydia,' Tuck said immediately. 'I never got to orbit the Earth or walk on the Moon. But I've just been places where no man has ever gone before. I've *done* things, *seen* things, Lydia, that have opened my eyes to a lot of things. To you . . . to life . . . to *everything*.'

He seemed to run out of steam. Lydia peered hard at him. 'Tuck, what are you trying to say?'

'It's not too late for me, Lydia. I can change. I can be better. I'm a different man already, I promise you.' He peered through the observation window at Jack, then looked back at her. 'I've known all along. Why couldn't I just admit it to myself?'

'Admit what, Tuck?'

'That I'm in love with you, of course.'

Lydia stared back at him, hardly believing what she had heard. A smile broke out on her lips.

'Boy . . .' she said.

'Let's get married.'

'Married?'

'Don't you want to?'

Lydia's smile broadened, and she flung her arms around his neck.

They hugged one another hard, and kissed. Then, through the window, Lydia saw Jack turning away sadly. Breaking the clinch, she rushed into the lab after him. He was heading for the door.

'Jack,' she said. 'Wait . . .'

He turned, and he was smiling, too.

'Lydia,' he said, 'you don't have to say a word. I'm happy for you and Tuck. I really am. This has been the most exciting twenty-four hours of my life. I've been chased, kidnapped, frozen, electrified, amplified and terrorized – *and I feel great!*'

13

From inside the church, an organ played the wedding march. The church doors opened, and out stepped Tuck and Lydia as the guests began to toss rice over their heads.

Among the guests were Dr Niles, Pete Blanchard, Duane Flornoy, Dr Greenbush, Mr Wormwood and Wendy. Jack, dressed in smart tuxedo, had been best man, and neither Tuck nor Lydia had had any objections to him inviting some of his closest acquaintances.

A long limousine awaited the wedding couple outside the church. After a hurried session of photographs and back-slapping, Jack managed to get a moment alone with Lydia and Tuck.

'Thanks for the cruise tickets, buddy,' Tuck said to him.

'Just take good care of Lydia for me,' he replied.

'I will. And you take good care of my car.'

Jack nodded. To both Tuck and Lydia, he said, 'We made one hell of a team, didn't we?'

'The best,' Lydia said. And she reached up to kiss him full on the lips.

A chauffeur approached the limousine with two heavy suitcases. He wore a pair of dark sunglasses, and his peaked cap was pulled down over his eyes. He opened the back of the car and put the suitcases inside.

Tuck and Lydia climbed into the back seat.

'Nobody noticed my cuff-links,' Tuck remarked.

Lydia frowned, not understanding, until she saw that they had been made of the two microchips.

'Tuck,' she said, grinning. 'You're incorrigible.'

At the back of the car, the chauffeur was arranging the suitcases in the trunk. Then, after a swift glance around to ensure that no one was watching him, he opened one of the cases.

Nestled among Lydia's clothing was Margaret Canker. The chauffeur opened the second case. Scrimshaw was inside, sitting on one of Tuck's shirts.

'He has the chips on him,' the chauffeur whispered to the two of them.

'Good, good!' said Scrimshaw. 'Close the lids before anyone sees us!'

'I can't breathe in here!' Canker complained.

'Shut up, Margaret!' said Scrimshaw.

The chauffeur snapped the suitcases shut and closed the trunk before climbing into the limousine. Neither Tuck nor Lydia had noticed that he was wearing cowboy boots.

'Don't run any red lights,' Jack told him as he drove off while the guests cheered and waved.

Jack watched the car drive away. Dr Greenbush appeared beside him.

'Nice wedding,' Greenbush remarked. 'Come around to my office next week, Jack. I'd like to run some new tests.'

Wormwood now came up. 'Since you're not taking that cruise now, Jack, I sure could use you down at the store on Monday.'

Jack backed away. Then Wendy appeared.

'I think we should try dating,' she said to him. 'Not *exclusively*, though . . . at least not for me.'

140

Jack was scarcely listening to any of them. He had been watching the chauffeur as he climbed into the limousine. There was something funny about him. Suddenly Jack realized what.

'Cowboy boots!' he cried. 'That was the Cowboy!'

The other three regarded him with perplexed surprise. Tuck's Mustang was parked at the kerb close by, and Jack had the keys in his pocket.

'Doc,' he said to Greenbush, 'I'm cured. Mr Wormwood – I quit. Wendy – not a chance!'

Then he raced off, vaulting into the Mustang without even opening the door. He slipped the keys into the ignition, and the engine started with a roar. All of his old fears and uncertainties were gone now. He was determined to take life by the scruff of the neck, to become master of his own destiny. And what better way to start than by going to Tuck and Lydia's aid right now?

'Jack Putter to the rescue!' he yelled as the Mustang shot off down the road in pursuit of the limousine.

Colour illustrated storybooks for the young reader

Help Your Child to Read
Allan Ahlberg and Eric Hill

Fast Frog	85p	☐
Bad Bear	85p	☐
Double Ducks	85p	☐
Poorly Pig	85p	☐
Rubber Rabbit	85p	☐
Silly Sheep	85p	☐

Allan Ahlberg and André Amstutz

Mister Wolf	85p	☐
Travelling Moose	85p	☐
Hip-Hippo Ray	85p	☐
King Kangaroo	85p	☐
Tell-Tale Tiger	85p	☐
Spider Spy	85p	☐

Help Your Child to Count
Richard & Nicky Hales and André Amstutz

Slimy Slugs	95p	☐
Captain Caterpillar	95p	☐
Furry Foxes	95p	☐
Boris Bat	95p	☐
Panda Picnic	95p	☐
Froggy Football	95p	☐

Rub A Dub Dub
Alan Rogers

Yankee Doodle	95p	☐
Three Men in a Tub	95p	☐
One for the Money	95p	☐
Tom, Tom the Piper's Son	95p	☐
Hey Diddle Diddle	95p	☐
Poor Old Robinson Crusoe	95p	☐

To order direct from the publisher just tick the titles you want
and fill in the order form.

All these books are available at your local bookshop or newsagent, or can be ordered direct from the publisher.

To order direct from the publishers just tick the titles you want and fill in the form below.

Name _____

Address _____

_____

Send to:
Dragon Cash Sales
PO Box 11, Falmouth, Cornwall TR10 9EN.

Please enclose remittance to the value of the cover price plus:

UK 45p for the first book, 20p for the second book plus 14p per copy for each additional book ordered to a maximum charge of £1.63.

BFPO and Eire 45p for the first book, 20p for the second book plus 14p per copy for the next 7 books, thereafter 8p per book.

Overseas 75p for the first book and 21p for each additional book.

Dragon Books reserve the right to show new retail prices on covers, which may differ from those previously advertised in the text or elsewhere.